Alfred Tennyson

Collection of british authors: The Poetical Works of Alfred Tennyson

Volume II.

Alfred Tennyson

Collection of british authors: The Poetical Works of Alfred Tennyson
Volume II.

ISBN/EAN: 9783742801661

Manufactured in Europe, USA, Canada, Australia, Japa

Cover: Foto ©Andreas Hilbeck / pixelio.de

Manufactured and distributed by brebook publishing software
(www.brebook.com)

Alfred Tennyson

Collection of british authors: The Poetical Works of Alfred Tennyson

COLLECTION

OF

BRITISH AUTHORS.

VOL. 502.

THE POETICAL WORKS OF TENNYSON.

VOL. II.

THE
POETICAL WORKS

OF

ALFRED TENNYSON

COPYRIGHT EDITION.

VOL. II.

IN MEMORIAM. — THE PRINCESS

LEIPZIG

BERNHARD TAUCHNITZ

1860.

IN MEMORIAM

BY

ALFRED TENNYSON.

Strong Son of God, immortal Love,
      Whom we, that have not seen thy face,
      By faith, and faith alone, embrace,
Believing where we cannot prove;

Thine are these orbs of light and shade;
      Thou madest Life in man and brute;
      Thou madest Death; and lo, thy foot
Is on the skull which thou hast made.

Thou wilt not leave us in the dust:
      Thou madest man, he knows not why;
      He thinks he was not made to die;
And thou hast made him: thou art just.

Thou seemest human and divine,
      The highest, holiest manhood, thou:
      Our wills are ours, we know not how;
Our wills are ours, to make them thine.
                                    1*

Our little systems have their day;
    They have their day and cease to be:
    They are but broken lights of thee,
And thou, O Lord, art more than they.

We have but faith: we cannot know;
    For knowledge is of things we see;
    And yet we trust it comes from thee,
A beam in darkness: let it grow.

Let knowledge grow from more to more,
    But more of reverence in us dwell;
    That mind and soul, according well,
May make one music as before,

But vaster.   We are fools and slight;
    We mock thee when we do not fear:
    But help thy foolish ones to bear;
Help thy vain worlds to bear thy light.

Forgive what seem'd my sin in me;
    What seem'd my worth since I began;
    For merit lives from man to man,
And not from man, O Lord, to thee.

Forgive my grief for one removed,
    Thy creature, whom I found so fair
    I trust he lives in thee, and there
I find him worthier to be loved.

Forgive these wild and wandering cries,
    Confusions of a wasted youth;
    Forgive them where they fail in truth,
And in thy wisdom make me wise.

                    1849.

IN MEMORIAM

A. H. H.

OBIIT MDCCCXXXIII.

I.

I HELD it truth, with him who sings
      To one clear harp in divers tones,
      That men may rise on stepping-stones
Of their dead selves to higher things.

But who shall so forecast the years
      And find in loss a gain to match?
      Or reach a hand thro' time to catch
The far-off interest of tears?

Let Love clasp Grief lest both be drown'd,
      Let darkness keep her raven gloss:
      Ah, sweeter to be drunk with loss,
To dance with death, to beat the ground,

Than that the victor Hours should scorn
      The long result of love, and boast,
      "Behold the man that loved and lost,
But all he was is overworn."

II.

Old Yew, which graspest at the stones
    That name the under-lying dead,
    Thy fibres net the dreamless head,
Thy roots are wrapt about the bones.

The seasons bring the flower again,
    And bring the firstling to the flock;
    And in the dusk of thee, the clock
Beats out the little lives of men.

O not for thee the glow, the bloom,
    Who changest not in any gale,
    Nor branding summer suns avail
To touch thy thousand years of gloom:

And gazing on thee, sullen tree,
    Sick for thy stubborn hardihood,
    I seem to fail from out my blood
And grow incorporate into thee.

III.

O sorrow, cruel fellowship,
    O Priestess in the vaults of Death,
    O sweet and bitter in a breath,
What whispers from thy lying lip?

"The stars," she whispers, "blindly run;
    A web is wov'n across the sky;
    From out waste places comes a cry
And murmurs from the dying sun:

"And all the phantom, Nature, stands —
    With all the music in her tone,
    A hollow echo of my own, —
A hollow form with empty hands."

And shall I take a thing so blind,
    Embrace her as my natural good;
    Or crush her, like a vice of blood,
Upon the threshold of the mind?

IV.

To Sleep I give my powers away;
    My will is bondsman to the dark;
    I sit within a helmless bark,
And with my heart I muse and say:

O heart, how fares it with thee now,
    That thou should'st fail from thy desire,
    Who scarcely darest to inquire,
"What is it makes me beat so low?"

Something it is which thou hast lost,
    Some pleasure from thine early years.
    Break, thou deep vase of chilling tears,
That grief hath shaken into frost!

Such clouds of nameless trouble cross
    All night below the darken'd eyes;
    With morning wakes the will, and cries,
"Thou shalt not be the fool of loss."

V.

I SOMETIMES hold it half a sin
    To put in words the grief I feel;
    For words, like Nature, half reveal
And half conceal the Soul within.

But, for the unquiet heart and brain,
    A use in measured language lies;
    The sad mechanic exercise,
Like dull narcotics, numbing pain.

In words, like weeds, I'll wrap me o'er,
    Like coarsest clothes against the cold;
    But that large grief which these enfold
Is given in outline and no more.

VI.

One writes, that "Other friends remain,"
     That "Loss is common to the race" —
     And common is the commonplace,
And vacant chaff well meant for grain.

That loss is common would not make
     My own less bitter, rather more:
     Too common! Never morning wore
To evening, but some heart did break.

O father, wheresoe'er thou be,
     Who pledgest now thy gallant son;
     A shot, ere half thy draught be done,
Hath still'd the life that beat from thee.

O mother, praying God will save
     Thy sailor, — while thy head is bow'd,
     His heavy-shotted hammock-shroud
Drops in his vast and wandering grave.

Ye know no more than I who wrought
     At that last hour to please him well;
     Who mused on all I had to tell,
And something written, something thought;

Expecting still his advent home;
      And ever met him on his way
      With wishes, thinking, here to-day,
Or here to-morrow will he come.

O somewhere, meek unconscious dove,
      That sittest ranging golden hair;
      And glad to find thyself so fair,
Poor child, that waitest for thy love!

For now her father's chimney glows
      In expectation of a guest;
      And thinking "this will please him best,"
She takes a riband or a rose;

For he will see them on to-night;
      And with the thought her colour burns;
      And, having left the glass, she turns
Once more to set a ringlet right;

And, even when she turn'd, the curse
      Had fallen, and her future Lord
      Was drown'd in passing thro' the ford,
Or kill'd in falling from his horse.

O what to her shall be the end?
      And what to me remains of good?
      To her, perpetual maidenhood,
And unto me no second friend.

VII.

Dark house, by which once more I stand
Here in the long unlovely street,
Doors, where my heart was used to beat
So quickly, waiting for a hand,

A hand that can be clasp'd no more —
Behold me, for I cannot sleep,
And like a guilty thing I creep
At earliest morning to the door.

He is not here; but far away
The noise of life begins again,
And ghastly thro' the drizzling rain
On the bald street breaks the blank day.

VIII.

A happy lover who has come
    To look on her that loves him well,
    Who 'lights and rings the gateway bell,
And learns her gone and far from home;

He saddens, all the magic light
    Dies off at once from bower and hall,
    And all the place is dark, and all
The chambers emptied of delight:

So find I every pleasant spot
    In which we two were wont to meet,
    The field, the chamber and the street,
For all is dark where thou art not.

Yet as that other, wandering there
    In those deserted walks, may find
    A flower beat with rain and wind,
Which once she foster'd up with care;

So seems it in my deep regret,
    O my forsaken heart, with thee
    And this poor flower of poesy
Which little cared for fades not yet.

But since it pleased a vanish'd eye,
    I go to plant it on his tomb,
    That if it can it there may bloom,
Or dying, there at least may die.

IX.

Fair ship, that from the Italian shore
    Sailest the placid ocean-plains
    With my lost Arthur's loved remains,
Spread thy full wings, and waft him o'er.

So draw him home to those that mourn
    In vain; a favourable speed
    Ruffle thy mirror'd mast, and lead
Thro' prosperous floods his holy urn.

All night no ruder air perplex
    Thy sliding keel, till Phosphor, bright
    As our pure love, thro' early light
Shall glimmer on the dewy decks.

Sphere all your lights around, above;
    Sleep, gentle heavens, before the prow;
    Sleep, gentle winds, as he sleeps now,
My friend, the brother of my love;

My Arthur, whom I shall not see
    Till all my widow'd race be run;
    Dear as the mother to the son,
More than my brothers are to me.

X.

I HEAR the noise about thy keel;
    I hear the bell struck in the night;
    I see the cabin-window bright;
I see the sailor at the wheel.

Thou bringest the sailor to his wife,
    And travell'd men from foreign lands;
    And letters unto trembling hands;
And, thy dark freight, a vanish'd life.

So bring him: we have idle dreams:
    This look of quiet flatters thus
    Our home-bred fancies: O to us,
The fools of habit, sweeter seems

To rest beneath the clover sod,
    That takes the sunshine and the rains,
    Or where the kneeling hamlet drains
The chalice of the grapes of God;

Than if with thee the roaring wells
    Should gulf him fathom-deep in brine;
    And hands so often clasp'd in mine,
Should toss with tangle and with shells.

XI.

Calm is the morn without a sound,
    Calm as to suit a calmer grief,
    And only thro' the faded leaf
The chesnut pattering to the ground:

Calm and deep peace on this high wold,
    And on these dews that drench the furze,
    And all the silvery gossamers
That twinkle into green and gold:

Calm and still light on yon great plain
    That sweeps with all its autumn bowers,
    And crowded farms and lessening towers,
To mingle with the bounding main:

Calm and deep peace in this wide air,
    These leaves that redden to the fall;
    And in my heart, if calm at all,
If any calm, a calm despair:

Calm on the seas, and silver sleep,
    And waves that sway themselves in rest,
    And dead calm in that noble breast
Which heaves but with the heaving deep.

XII.

Lo, as a dove when up she springs
    To bear thro' Heaven a tale of woe,
    Some dolorous message knit below
The wild pulsation of her wings;

Like her I go; I cannot stay;
    I leave this mortal ark behind,
    A weight of nerves without a mind,
And leave the cliffs, and haste away

O'er ocean-mirrors rounded large,
    And reach the glow of southern skies,
    And see the sails at distance rise,
And linger weeping on the marge,

And saying; "Comes he thus, my friend?
    Is this the end of all my care?"
    And circle moaning in the air:
"Is this the end? Is this the end?"

And forward dart again, and play
    About the prow, and back return
    To where the body sits, and learn,
That I have been an hour away.

XIII.

TEARS of the widower, when he sees
    A late-lost form that sleep reveals,
    And moves his doubtful arms, and feels
Her place is empty, fall like these;

Which weep a loss for ever new,
    A void where heart on heart reposed;
    And, where warm hands have prest and closed,
Silence, till I be silent too.

Which weep the comrade of my choice,
    An awful thought, a life removed,
    The human-hearted man I loved,
A Spirit, not a breathing voice.

Come Time, and teach me, many years,
    I do not suffer in a dream;
    For now so strange do these things seem,
Mine eyes have leisure for their tears;

My fancies time to rise on wing,
    And glance about the approaching sails,
    As tho' they brought but merchants' bales,
And not the burthen that they bring.

XIV.

If one should bring me this report,
    That thou hadst touch'd the land to-day,
    And I went down unto the quay,
And found thee lying in the port;

And standing, muffled round with woe,
    Should see thy passengers in rank
    Come stepping lightly down the plank,
And beckoning unto those they know;

And if along with these should come
    The man I held as half-divine;
    Should strike a sudden hand in mine,
And ask a thousand things of home;

And I should tell him all my pain,
    And how my life had droop'd of late,
    And he should sorrow o'er my state
And marvel what possess'd my brain;

And I perceived no touch of change,
    No hint of death in all his frame,
    But found him all in all the same,
I should not feel it to be strange.

XV.

To-night the winds begin to rise
  And roar from yonder dropping day:
  The last red leaf is whirl'd away,
The rooks are blown about the skies;

The forest crack'd, the waters curl'd,
  The cattle huddled on the lea;
  And wildly dash'd on tower and tree
The sunbeam strikes along the world:

And but for fancies, which aver
  That all thy motions gently pass
  Athwart a plane of molten glass,
I scarce could brook the strain and stir

That makes the barren branches loud;
  And but for fear it is not so,
  The wild unrest that lives in woe
Would dote and pore on yonder cloud

That rises upward always higher,
  And onward drags a labouring breast,
  And topples round the dreary west,
A looming bastion fringed with fire.

XVL

WHAT words are these have fall'n from me?
    Can calm despair and wild unrest
    Be tenants of a single breast,
Or sorrow such a changeling be?

Or doth she only seem to take
    The touch of change in calm or storm;
    But knows no more of transient form
In her deep self, than some dead lake

That holds the shadow of a lark
    Hung in the shadow of a heaven?
    Or has the shock, so harshly given,
Confused me like the unhappy bark

That strikes by night a craggy shelf,
    And staggers blindly ere she sink?
    And stunn'd me from my power to think
And all my knowledge of myself;

And made me that delirious man
    Whose fancy fuses old and new,
    And flashes into false and true,
And mingles all without a plan?

XVII.

Thou comest, much wept for: such a breeze
　　Compell'd thy canvas, and my prayer
　　Was as the whisper of an air
To breathe thee over lonely seas.

For I in spirit saw thee move
　　Thro' circles of the bounding sky,
　　Week after week: the days go by:
Come quick, thou bringest all I love.

Henceforth, wherever thou may'st roam,
　　My blessing, like a line of light,
　　Is on the waters day and night,
And like a beacon guards thee home.

So may whatever tempest mars
　　Mid-ocean, spare thee, sacred bark;
　　And balmy drops in summer dark
Slide from the bosom of the stars.

So kind an office hath been done,
　　Such precious relics brought by thee;
　　The dust of him I shall not see
Till all my widow'd race be run.

XVIII.

'Tis well; 'tis something; we may stand
    Where he in English earth is laid,
    And from his ashes may be made
The violet of his native land.

'Tis little; but it looks in truth
    As if the quiet bones were blest
    Among familiar names to rest
And in the places of his youth.

Come then, pure hands, and bear the head
    That sleeps or wears the mask of sleep,
    And come, whatever loves to weep,
And hear the ritual of the dead.

Ah yet, ev'n yet, if this might be,
    I, falling on his faithful heart,
    Would breathing thro' his lips impart
The life that almost dies in me;

That dies not, but endures with pain,
    And slowly forms the firmer mind,
    Treasuring the look it cannot find,
The words that are not heard again.

XIX.

The Danube to the Severn gave
    The darken'd heart that beat no more;
    They laid him by the pleasant shore,
And in the hearing of the wave.

There twice a day the Severn fills;
    The salt sea-water passes by,
    And hushes half the babbling Wye,
And makes a silence in the hills.

The Wye is hush'd nor moved along,
    And hush'd my deepest grief of all,
    When fill'd with tears that cannot fall,
I brim with sorrow drowning song.

The tide flows down, the wave again
    Is vocal in its wooded walls;
    My deeper anguish also falls,
And I can speak a little then.

XX.

THE lesser griefs that may be said,
    That breathe a thousand tender vows,
    Are but as servants in a house
Where lies the master newly dead;

Who speak their feeling as it is,
    And weep the fullness from the mind:
    "It will be hard" they say "to find
Another service such as this."

My lighter moods are like to these,
    That out of words a comfort win;
    But there are other griefs within,
And tears that at their fountain freeze;

For by the hearth the children sit
    Cold in that atmosphere of Death,
    And scarce endure to draw the breath,
Or like to noiseless phantoms flit:

But open converse is there none,
    So much the vital spirits sink
    To see the vacant chair, and think,
"How good! how kind! and he is gone."

XXL.

I sing to him that rests below,
    And, since the grasses round me wave,
    I take the grasses of the grave,
And make them pipes whereon to blow.

The traveller hears me now and then,
    And sometimes harshly will he speak;
    "This fellow would make weakness weak,
And 'melt the waxen hearts of men."

Another answers, "Let him be,
    He loves to make parade of pain,
    That with his piping he may gain
The praise that comes to constancy."

A third is wroth, "Is this an hour
    For private sorrow's barren song,
    When more and more the people throng
The chairs and thrones of civil power?

A time to sicken and to swoon,
    When Science reaches forth her arms
    To feel from world to world, and charms
Her secret from the latest moon?"

Behold, ye speak an idle thing:
    Ye never knew the sacred dust:
    I do but sing because I must,
And pipe but as the linnets sing:

And one is glad; her note is gay,
    For now her little ones have ranged;
    And one is sad; her note is changed,
Because her brood is stol'n away.

XXII.

The path by which we twain did go,
      Which led by tracts that pleased us well,
      Thro' four sweet years arose and fell,
From flower to flower, from snow to snow:

And we with singing cheer'd the way,
      And crown'd with all the season lent,
      From April on to April went,
And glad at heart from May to May:

But where the path we walk'd began
      To slant the fifth autumnal slope,
      As we descended following Hope,
There sat the Shadow fear'd of man;

Who broke our fair companionship,
      And spread his mantle dark and cold,
      And wrapt thee formless in the fold,
And dull'd the murmur on thy lip,

And bore thee where I could not see
      Nor follow, tho' I walk in haste,
      And think, that somewhere in the waste
The Shadow sits and waits for me.

XXIII.

Now, sometimes in my sorrow shut,
    Or breaking into song by fits,
    Alone, alone, to where he sits,
The Shadow cloak'd from head to foot,

Who keeps the keys of all the creeds,
    I wander, often falling lame,
    And looking back to whence I came,
Or on to where the pathway leads;

And crying, "how changed from where it ran
    Thro' lands where not a leaf was dumb;
    But all the lavish hills would hum
The murmur of a happy Pan:

When each by turns was guide to each,
    And Fancy light from Fancy caught,
    And Thought leapt out to wed with Thought,
Ere Thought could wed itself with Speech;

And all we met was fair and good,
    And all was good that Time could bring,
    And all the secret of the Spring
Moved in the chambers of the blood;

And many an old philosophy
    On Argive heights divinely sang,
    And round us all the thicket rang
To many a flute of Arcady."

XXIV.

And was the day of my delight
　　As pure and perfect as I say?
　　The very source and fount of Day
Is dash'd with wandering isles of night.

If all was good and fair we met,
　　This earth had been the Paradise
　　It never look'd to human eyes
Since Adam left his garden yet.

And is it that the haze of grief
　　Makes former gladness loom so great?
　　The lowness of the present state,
That sets the past in this relief?

Or that the past will always win
　　A glory from its being far;
　　And orb into the perfect star
We saw not, when we moved therein?

XIV.

I know that this was Life, — the track
    Whereon with equal feet we fared;
    And then, as now, the day prepared
The daily burden for the back.

But this it was that made me move
    As light as carrier-birds in air;
    I loved the weight I had to bear,
Because it needed help of Love:

Nor could I weary, heart or limb,
    When mighty Love would cleave in twain
    The lading of a single pain,
And part it, giving half to him.

XXVI.

Still onward winds the dreary way;
    I with it; for I long to prove
    No lapse of moons can canker Love
Whatever fickle tongues may say.

And if that eye which watches guilt
    And goodness, and hath power to see
    Within the green the moulder'd tree,
And towers fall'n as soon as built —

Oh, if indeed that eye foresee
    Or see (in Him is no before)
    In more of life true life no more,
And Love the indifference to be, ·

Then might I find, ere yet the morn
    Breaks hither over Indian seas,
    That Shadow waiting with the keys,
To shroud me from my proper scorn.

XXVII.

I ENVY not in any moods
    The captive void of noble rage,
    The linnet born within the cage,
That never knew the summer woods:

I envy not the beast that takes
    His license in the field of time,
    Unfetter'd by the sense of crime
To whom a conscience never wakes;

Nor, what may count itself as blest,
    The heart that never plighted troth
    But stagnates in the weeds of sloth;
Nor any want-begotten rest.

I hold it true, whate'er befall;
    I feel it, when I sorrow most;
    'Tis better to have loved and lost
Than never to have loved at all.

XXVIII.

THE time draws near the birth of Christ:
    The moon is hid; the night is still;
    The Christmas bells from hill to hill
Answer each other in the mist.

Four voices of four hamlets round,
    From far and near, on mead and moor,
    Swell out and fail, as if a door
Were shut between me and the sound:

Each voice four changes on the wind,
    That now dilate, and now decrease,
    Peace and goodwill, goodwill and peace,
Peace and goodwill, to all mankind.

This year I slept and woke with pain,
    I almost wish'd no more to wake,
    And that my hold on life would break
Before I heard those bells again:

But they my troubled spirit rule,
    For they controll'd me when a boy;
    They bring me sorrow touch'd with joy,
The merry merry bells of Yule.

XXIX.

With such compelling cause to grieve
    As daily vexes household peace,
    And chains regret to his decease,
How dare we keep our Christmas-eve;

Which brings no more a welcome guest
    To enrich the threshold of the night
    With shower'd largess of delight,
In dance and song and game and jest.

Yet go, and while the holly boughs
    Entwine the cold baptismal font,
    Make one wreath more for Use and Wont,
That guard the portals of the house;

Old sisters of a day gone by,
    Gray nurses, loving nothing new;
    Why should they miss their yearly due
Before their time? They too will die.

XXX.

With trembling fingers did we weave
      The holly round the Christmas hearth;
      A rainy cloud possess'd the earth,
And sadly fell our Christmas-eve.

At our old pastimes in the hall
      We gambol'd, making vain pretence
      Of gladness, with an awful sense
Of one mute Shadow watching all.

We paused: the winds were in the beech:
      We heard them sweep the winter land;
      And in a circle hand-in-hand
Sat silent, looking each at each.

Then echo-like our voices rang;
      We sung, tho' every eye was dim,
      A merry song we sang with him
Last year: impetuously we sang:

We ceased: a gentler feeling crept
      Upon us: surely rest is meet:
      "They rest," we said, "their sleep is sweet,"
And silence follow'd, and we wept.

Our voices took a higher range;
      Once more we sang: "They do not die
      Nor lose their mortal sympathy,
Nor change to us, although they change;

Rapt from the fickle and the frail
      With gather'd power, yet the same,
      Pierces the keen seraphic flame
From orb to orb, from veil to veil."

Rise, happy morn, rise, holy morn,
      Draw forth the cheerful day from night:
      O Father, touch the east, and light
The light that shone when Hope was born.

XXXI.

WHEN Lazarus left his charnel-cave,
    And home to Mary's house return'd,
    Was this demanded — if he yearn'd
To hear her weeping by his grave?

"Where wert thou, brother, those four days?"
    There lives no record of reply,
    Which telling what it is to die
Had surely added praise to praise.

From every house the neighbours met,
    The streets were fill'd with joyful sound,
    A solemn gladness even crown'd
The purple brows of Olivet.

Behold a man raised up by Christ!
    The rest remaineth unreveal'd;
    He told it not; or something seal'd
The lips of that Evangelist.

XXXII.

Her eyes are homes of silent prayer,
    Nor other thought her mind admits
    But, he was dead, and there he sits
And he that brought him back is there.

Then one deep love doth supersede
    All other, when her ardent gaze
    Roves from the living brother's face,
And rests upon the Life indeed.

All subtle thought, all curious fears,
    Borne down by gladness so complete,
    She bows, she bathes the Saviour's feet
With costly spikenard and with tears.

Thrice blest whose lives are faithful prayers,
    Whose loves in higher love endure;
    What souls possess themselves so pure,
Or is there blessedness like theirs?

XXXIII.

O THOU that after toil and storm
　　Mayst seem to have reach'd a purer air,
　　Whose faith has centre everywhere,
Nor cares to fix itself to form,

Leave thou thy sister when she prays,
　　Her early Heaven, her happy views;
　　Nor thou with shadow'd hint confuse
A life that leads melodious days.

Her faith thro' form is pure as thine,
　　Her hands are quicker unto good:
　　Oh, sacred be the flesh and blood
To which she links a truth divine!

See thou, that countest reason ripe
　　In holding by the law within,
　　Thou fail not in a world of sin,
And ev'n for want of such a type.

LXXIV.

My own dim life should teach me this,
    That life shall live for evermore,
    Else earth is darkness at the core,
And dust and ashes all that is;

This round of green, this orb of flame,
    Fantastic beauty; such as lurks
    In some wild Poet, when he works
Without a conscience or an aim.

What then were God to such as I?
    'Twere hardly worth my while to choose
    Of things all mortal, or to use
A little patience ere I die;

'Twere best at once to sink to peace,
    Like birds the charming serpent draws,
    To drop head-foremost in the jaws
Of vacant darkness and to cease.

XXXV.

Yet if some voice that man could trust
    Should murmur from the narrow house,
    "The cheeks drop in; the body bows;
Man dies: nor is there hope in dust:"

Might I not say? "yet even here,
    But for one hour, O Love, I strive
    To keep so sweet a thing alive:"
But I should turn mine ears and hear

The moanings of the homeless sea,
    The sound of streams that swift or slow
    Draw down Æonian hills, and sow
The dust of continents to be;

And Love would answer with a sigh,
    "The sound of that forgetful shore
    Will change my sweetness more and more,
Half-dead to know that I shall die."

O me, what profits it to put
    An idle case? If Death were seen
    At first as Death, Love had not been,
Or been in narrowest working shut,

More fellowship of sluggish moods,
    Or in his coarsest Satyr-shape
    Had bruised the herb and crush'd the grape,
And bask'd and batten'd in the woods.

XXXVI.

Tho' truths in manhood darkly join,
    Deep-seated in our mystic frame,
    We yield all blessing to the name
Of Him that made them current coin;

For Wisdom dealt with mortal powers,
    Where truth in closest words shall fail,
    When truth embodied in a tale
Shall enter in at lowly doors.

And so the Word had breath, and wrought
    With human hands the creed of creeds
    In loveliness of perfect deeds,
More strong than all poetic thought;

Which he may read that binds the sheaf,
    Or builds the house, or digs the grave,
    And those wild eyes that watch the wave
In roarings round the coral reef.

XXXVII.

Urania speaks with darken'd brow:
    "Thou pratest here where thou art least;
    This faith has many a purer priest,
And many an abler voice than thou.

Go down beside thy native rill,
    On thy Parnassus set thy feet,
    And hear thy laurel whisper sweet
About the ledges of the hill."

And my Melpomene replies,
    A touch of shame upon her cheek:
    "I am not worthy ev'n to speak
Of thy prevailing mysteries;

For I am but an earthly Muse,
    And owning but a little art
    To lull with song an aching heart,
And render human love his dues;

But brooding on the dear one dead,
    And all he said of things divine,
    (And dear to me as sacred wine
To dying lips is all he said),

I murmur'd, as I came along,
    Of comfort clasp'd in truth reveal'd;
    And loiter'd in the master's field,
And darken'd sanctities with song."

XXXVIII.

With weary steps I loiter on,
    Tho' always under alter'd skies
    The purple from the distance dies,
My prospect and horizon gone.

No joy the blowing season gives,
    The herald melodies of spring,
    But in the songs I love to sing
A doubtful gleam of solace lives.

If any care for what is here
    Survive in spirits render'd free,
    Then are these songs I sing of thee
Not all ungrateful to thine ear.

XXXIX.

Could we forget the widow'd hour
    And look on Spirits breathed away,
    As on a maiden in the day
When first she wears her orange-flower!

When crown'd with blessing she doth rise
    To take her latest leave of home,
    And hopes and light regrets that come
Make April of her tender eyes;

And doubtful joys the father move,
    And tears are on the mother's face,
    As parting with a long embrace
She enters other realms of love;

Her office there to rear, to teach,
    Becoming as is meet and fit
    A link among the days, to knit
The generations each with each;

And, doubtless, unto thee is given
    A life that bears immortal fruit
    In such great offices as suit
The full-grown energies of heaven.

Ay me, the difference I discern!
    How often shall her old fireside
    Be cheer'd with tidings of the bride,
How often she herself return,

And tell them all they would have told,
    And bring her babe, and make her boast,
    'Till even those that miss'd her most,
Shall count new things as dear as old:

But thou and I have shaken hands,
    'Till growing winters lay me low;
    My paths are in the fields I know,
And thine in undiscover'd lands.

XL.

Thy spirit ere our fatal loss
    Did ever rise from high to higher;
    As mounts the heavenward altar-fire,
As flies the lighter thro' the gross.

But thou art turn'd to something strange,
    And I have lost the links that bound
    Thy changes; here upon the ground,
No more partaker of thy change.

Deep folly! yet that this could be —
    That I could wing my will with might
    To leap the grades of life and light,
And flash at once, my friend, to thee:

For tho' my nature rarely yields
    To that vague fear implied in death;
    Nor shudders at the gulfs beneath,
The howlings from forgotten fields;

Yet oft when sundown skirts the moor
    An inner trouble I behold,
    A spectral doubt which makes me cold,
That I shall be thy mate no more,

Tho' following with an upward mind
    The wonders that have come to thee,
    Thro' all the secular to-be,
But evermore a life behind.

XLI

I vex my heart with fancies dim:
    He still outstript me in the race;
    It was but unity of place
That made me dream I rank'd with him.

And so may Place retain us still,
    And he the much-beloved again,
    A lord of large experience, train
To riper growth the mind and will:

And what delights can equal those
    That stir the spirit's inner deeps,
    When one that loves but knows not, reaps
A truth from one that loves and knows?

XLII.

If Sleep and Death be truly one,
    And every spirit's folded bloom
    Thro' all its intervital gloom
In some long trance should slumber on;

Unconscious of the sliding hour,
    Bare of the body, might it last,
    And silent traces of the past
Be all the colour of the flower:

So then were nothing lost to man;
    So that still garden of the souls
    In many a figured leaf enrolls
The total world since life began;

And love will last as pure and whole
    As when he loved me here in Time,
    And at the spiritual prime
Rewaken with the dawning soul.

XLIII.

How fares it with the happy dead?
    For here the man is more and more;
    But he forgets the days before
God shut the doorways of his head.

The days have vanish'd, tone and tint,
    And yet perhaps the hoarding sense
    Gives out at times (he knows not whence)
A little flash, a mystic hint;

And in the long harmonious years
    (If Death so taste Lethean springs)
    May some dim touch of earthly things
Surprise thee ranging with thy peers.

If such a dreamy touch should fall,
    O turn thee round, resolve the doubt;
    My guardian angel will speak out
In that high place, and tell thee all.

XLIV.

THE baby new to earth and sky,
    What time his tender palm is prest
    Against the circle of the breast,
Has never thought that "this is I:"

But as he grows he gathers much,
    And learns the use of "I" and "me,"
    And finds "I am not what I see,
And other than the things I touch."

So rounds he to a separate mind
    From whence clear memory may begin,
    As thro' the frame that binds him in
His isolation grows defined.

This use may lie in blood and breath,
    Which else were fruitless of their due,
    Had man to learn himself anew
Beyond the second birth of Death.

XLV.

We ranging down this lower track,
    The path we came by, thorn and flower,
    Is shadow'd by the growing hour,
Lest life should fail in looking back.

So be it: there no shade can last
    In that deep dawn behind the tomb,
    But clear from marge to marge shall bloom
The eternal landscape of the past;

A lifelong tract of time reveal'd;
    The fruitful hours of still increase;
    Days order'd in a wealthy peace,
And those five years its richest field.

O Love, thy province were not large,
    A bounded field, nor stretching far;
    Look also, Love, a brooding star,
A rosy warmth from marge to marge.

XLVI.

That each, who seems a separate whole,
    Should move his rounds, and fusing all
    The skirts of self again, should fall
Remerging in the general Soul,

Is faith as vague as all unsweet:
    Eternal form shall still divide
    The eternal soul from all beside;
And I shall know him when we meet:

And we shall sit at endless feast,
    Enjoying each the other's good:
    What vaster dream can hit the mood
Of Love on earth? He seeks at least

Upon the last and sharpest height,
    Before the spirits fade away,
    Some landing-place, to clasp and say,
"Farewell! We lose ourselves in light."

XLVII.

If these brief lays, of Sorrow born,
    Were taken to be such as closed
    Grave doubts and answers here proposed,
Then these were such as men might scorn:

Her care is not to part and prove;
    She takes, when harsher moods remit,
    What slender shade of doubt may flit,
And makes it vassal unto love:

And hence, indeed, she sports with words,
    But better serves a wholesome law,
    And holds it sin and shame to draw
The deepest measure from the chords:

Nor dare she trust a larger lay,
    But rather looseus from the lip
    Short swallow-flights of song, that dip
Their wings in tears, and skim away.

XLVIII.

From art, from nature, from the schools,
　　Let random influences glance,
　　Like light in many a shiver'd lance
That breaks about the dappled pools:

The lightest wave of thought shall lisp,
　　The fancy's tenderest eddy wreathe,
　　The slightest air of song shall breathe
To make the sullen surface crisp.

And look thy look, and go thy way,
　　But blame not thou the winds that make
　　The seeming-wanton ripple break,
The tender-pencil'd shadow play.

Beneath all fancied hopes and fears
　　Ay me, the sorrow deepens down,
　　Whose muffled motions blindly drown
The bases of my life in tears.

XLIX.

Be near me when my light is low,
      When the blood creeps, and the nerves prick
      And tingle; and the heart is sick,
And all the wheels of Being slow.

Be near me when the sensuous frame
      Is rack'd with pangs that conquer trust;
      And Time, a maniac scattering dust,
And Life, a Fury slinging flame.

Be near me when my faith is dry,
      And men the flies of latter spring,
      That lay their eggs, and sting and sing,
And weave their petty cells and die.

Be near me when I fade away,
      To point the term of human strife,
      And on the low dark verge of life
The twilight of eternal day.

LI

Do we indeed desire the dead
　　Should still be near us at our side?
　　Is there no baseness we would hide?
No inner vileness that we dread?

Shall he for whose applause I strove,
　　I had such reverence for his blame,
　　See with clear eye some hidden shame
And I be lessen'd in his love?

I wrong the grave with fears untrue:
　　Shall love be blamed for want of faith?
　　There must be wisdom with great Death:
The dead shall look me thro' and thro'.

Be near us when we climb or fall:
　　Ye watch, like God, the rolling hours
　　With larger other eyes than ours,
To make allowance for us all.

LI.

I CANNOT love thee as I ought,
    For love reflects the thing beloved;
    My words are only words, and moved
Upon the topmost froth of thought.

"Yet blame not thou thy plaintive song,"
    The Spirit of true love replied;
    "Thou canst not move me from thy side,
Nor human frailty do me wrong.

"What keeps a spirit wholly true
    To that ideal which he bears?
    What record? not the sinless years
That breathed beneath the Syrian blue:

"So fret not, like an idle girl,
    That life is dash'd with flecks of sin.
    Abide: thy wealth is gather'd in,
When Time hath sunder'd shell from pearl."

LII.

How many a father have I seen,
     A sober man, among his boys,
     Whose youth was full of foolish noise,
Who wears his manhood halo and green:

And dare we to this fancy give,
     That had the wild oat not been sown,
     The soil, left barren, scarce had grown
The grain by which a man may live?

Oh, if we held the doctrine sound
     For life outliving heats of youth,
     Yet who would preach it as a truth
To those that eddy round and round?

Hold thou the good: define it well:
     For fear divine Philosophy
     Should push beyond her mark, and be
Procuress to the Lords of Hell.

LIII.

Oh yet we trust that somehow good
    Will be the final goal of ill,
    To pangs of nature, sins of will,
Defects of doubt, and taints of blood;

That nothing walks with aimless feet;
    That not one life shall be destroy'd,
    Or cast as rubbish to the void,
When God hath made the pile complete;

That not a worm is cloven in vain;
    That not a moth with vain desire
    Is shrivel'd in a fruitless fire,
Or but subserves another's gain.

Behold, we know not anything;
    I can but trust that good shall fall
    At last — far off — at last, to all,
And every winter change to spring.

So runs my dream: but what am I?
    An infant crying in the night:
    An infant crying for the light:
And with no language but a cry.

LIV.

The wish, that of the living whole
    No life may fail beyond the grave,
    Derives it not from what we have
The likest God within the soul?

Are God and Nature then at strife,
    That Nature lends such evil dreams?
    So careful of the type she seems,
So careless of the single life;

That I, considering everywhere
    Her secret meaning in her deeds,
    And finding that of fifty seeds
She often brings but one to bear,

I falter where I firmly trod,
    And falling with my weight of cares
    Upon the great world's altar-stairs
That slope thro' darkness up to God,

I stretch lame hands of faith, and grope,
    And gather dust and chaff, and call
    To what I feel is Lord of all,
And faintly trust the larger hope.

LV.

"So careful of the type?" but no.
From scarped cliff and quarried stone
She cries "a thousand types are gone:
I care for nothing, all shall go.

Thou makest thine appeal to me:
I bring to life, I bring to death:
'The spirit does but mean the breath:
I know no more." And he, shall he,

Man, her last work, who seem'd so fair,
Such splendid purpose in his eyes,
Who roll'd the psalm to wintry skies,
Who built him fanes of fruitless prayer,

Who trusted God was love indeed
And love Creation's final law —
Tho' Nature, red in tooth and claw
With ravine, shriek'd against his creed —

Who loved, who suffer'd countless ills,
Who battled for the True, the Just,
Be blown about the desert dust,
Or seal'd within the iron hills?

No more? A monster then, a dream,
  A discord. Dragons of the prime,
  That tare each other in their slime,
Were mellow music match'd with him.

O life as futile, then, as frail!
  O for thy voice to soothe and bless!
  What hope of answer, or redress?
Behind the veil, behind the veil.

LVI.

Peace; come away: the song of woe
    Is after all an earthly song:
    Peace; come away: we do him wrong
To sing so wildly: let us go.

Come; let us go: your cheeks are pale;
    But half my life I leave behind:
    Methinks my friend is richly shrined;
But I shall pass; my work will fail.

Yet in these ears, till hearing dies,
    One set slow bell will seem to toll
    The passing of the sweetest soul
That ever look'd with human eyes.

I hear it now, and o'er and o'er,
    Eternal greetings to the dead;
    And "Ave, Ave, Ave," said,
"Adieu, adieu" for evermore.

LVII.

In those sad words I took farewell:
    Like echoes in sepulchral halls,
    As drop by drop the water falls
In vaults and catacombs, they fell;

And, falling, idly broke the peace
    Of hearts that beat from day to day,
    Half-conscious of their dying clay,
And those cold crypts where they shall cease.

The high Muse answer'd: "Wherefore grieve
    Thy brethren with a fruitless tear?
    Abide a little longer here,
And thou shalt take a nobler leave."

LVIII.

O Sorrow, wilt thou live with me
    No casual mistress, but a wife,
    My bosom-friend and half of life;
As I confess it needs must be;

O Sorrow, wilt thou rule my blood,
    Be sometimes lovely like a bride,
    And put thy harsher moods aside,
If thou wilt have me wise and good.

My centred passion cannot move,
    Nor will it lessen from to-day;
    But I'll have leave at times to play
As with the creature of my love;

And set thee forth, for thou art mine,
    With so much hope for years to come,
    That, howsoe'er I know thee, some
Could hardly tell what name were thine.

LIX.

He past; a soul of nobler tone:
　　My spirit loved and loves him yet,
　　Like some poor girl whose heart is set
On one whose rank exceeds her own.

He mixing with his proper sphere,
　　She finds the baseness of her lot,
　　Half jealous of she knows not what,
And envying all that meet him there.

The little village looks forlorn;
　　She sighs amid her narrow days,
　　Moving about the household ways,
In that dark house where she was born.

The foolish neighbours come and go,
　　And tease her till the day draws by:
　　At night she weeps, "How vain am I!
How should he love a thing so low?"

LX.

Ir, in thy second state sublime,
    Thy ransom'd reason change replies
    With all the circle of the wise,
The perfect flower of human time;

And if thou cast thine eyes below,
    How dimly character'd and slight,
    How dwarf'd a growth of cold and night,
How blanch'd with darkness must I grow!

Yet turn thee to the doubtful shore,
    Where thy first form was made a man;
    I loved thee, Spirit, and love, nor can
The soul of Shakspeare love thee more.

LII.

Tho' if an eye that's downward cast
    Could make thee somewhat blench or fail,
    Then be my love an idle tale,
And fading legend of the past;

And thou, as one that once declined,
    When he was little more than boy,
    On some unworthy heart with joy,
But lives to wed an equal mind;

And breathes a novel world, the while
    His other passion wholly dies,
    Or in the light of deeper eyes
Is matter for a flying smile.

LXII.

Yet pity for a horse o'er-driven,
    And love in which my hound has part,
    Can hang no weight upon my heart
In its assumptions up to heaven;

And I am so much more than these,
    As thou, perchance, art more than I,
    And yet I spare them sympathy
And I would set their pains at ease.

So may'st thou watch me where I weep,
    As, unto vaster motions bound,
    The circuits of thine orbit round
A higher height, a deeper deep.

LXIII.

Dost thou look back on what hath been,
　　As some divinely gifted man,
　　Whose life in low estate began
And on a simple village green;

Who breaks his birth's invidious bar,
　　And grasps the skirts of happy chance,
　　And breasts the blows of circumstance,
And grapples with his evil star;

Who makes by force his merit known
　　And lives to clutch the golden keys,
　　To mould a mighty state's decrees,
And shape the whisper of the throne;

And moving up from high to higher,
　　Becomes on Fortune's crowning slope
　　The pillar of a people's hope,
The centre of a world's desire;

Yet feels, as in a pensive dream,
　　When all his active powers are still,
　　A distant dearness in the hill,
A secret sweetness in the stream,

The limit of his narrower fate,
    While yet beside its vocal springs
    He play'd at counsellors and kings,
With one that was his earliest mate;

Who ploughs with pain his native lea
    And reaps the labour of his hands,
    Or in the furrow musing stands;
"Does my old friend remember me?"

LXIV.

Sweet soul, do with me as thou wilt;
 I lull a fancy trouble-tost
 With "Love's too precious to be lost,
A little grain shall not be spilt."

And in that solace can I sing,
 Till out of painful phases wrought
 There flutters up a happy thought,
Self-balanced on a lightsome wing:

Since we deserved the name of friends,
 And thine effect so lives in me,
 A part of mine may live in thee,
And move thee on to noble ends.

LXV.

You thought my heart too far diseased;
    You wonder when my fancies play
    To find me gay among the gay,
Like one with any trifle pleased.

The shade by which my life was crost,
    Which makes a desert in the mind,
    Has made me kindly with my kind,
And like to him whose sight is lost;

Whose feet are guided thro' the land,
    Whose jest among his friends is free,
    Who takes the children on his knee,
And winds their curls about his hand:

He plays with threads, he beats his chair
    For pastime, dreaming of the sky;
    His inner day can never die,
His night of loss is always there.

LXVI.

WHEN on my bed the moonlight falls,
    I know that in thy place of rest
    By that broad water of the west,
There comes a glory on the walls:

Thy marble bright in dark appears,
    As slowly steals a silver flame
    Along the letters of thy name,
And o'er the number of thy years.

The mystic glory swims away;
    From off my bed the moonlight dies;
    And closing eaves of wearied eyes
I sleep till dusk is dipt in gray:

And then I know the mist is drawn
    A lucid veil from coast to coast,
    And in the dark church like a ghost
Thy tablet glimmers to the dawn.

LXVII.

When in the down I sink my head,
    Sleep, Death's twin-brother, times my breath;
    Sleep, Death's twin-brother, knows not Death,
Nor can I dream of thee as dead:

I walk as ere I walk'd forlorn,
    When all our path was fresh with dew,
    And all the bugle breezes blew
Reveillée to the breaking morn.

But what is this?   I turn about,
    I find a trouble in thine eye,
    Which makes me sad I know not why,
Nor can my dream resolve the doubt:

But ere the lark hath left the lea
    I wake, and I discern the truth;
    It is the trouble of my youth
That foolish sleep transfers to thee.

LXVIII.

I DREAM'D there would be Spring no more,
That Nature's ancient power was lost:
The streets were black with smoke and frost,
They chatter'd trifles at the door:

I wander'd from the noisy town,
I found a wood with thorny boughs:
I took the thorns to bind my brows,
I wore them like a civic crown:

I met with scoffs, I met with scorns
From youth and babe and hoary hairs:
They call'd me in the public squares
The fool that wears a crown of thorns:

They call'd me fool, they call'd me child:
I found an angel of the night;
The voice was low, the look was bright;
He look'd upon my crown and smiled:

He reach'd the glory of a hand,
That seem'd to touch it into leaf:
The voice was not the voice of grief;
The words were hard to understand.

LXIX.

I CANNOT see the features right,
     When on the gloom I strive to paint
     The face I know, the hues are faint
And mix with hollow masks of night;

Cloud-towers by ghostly masons wrought,
     A gulf that ever shuts and gapes,
     A hand that points, and palled shapes
In shadowy thoroughfares of thought;

And crowds that stream from yawning doors,
     And shoals of pucker'd faces drive;
     Dark bulks that tumble half alive,
And lazy lengths on boundless shores:

Till all at once beyond the will
     I hear a wizard music roll,
     And thro' a lattice on the soul
Looks thy fair face and makes it still.

LXX.

Sleep, kinsman thou to death and trance
　　And madness, thou hast forged at last
　　A night-long Present of the Past
In which we went thro' summer France.

Hadst thou such credit with the soul?
　　Then bring an opiate trebly strong,
　　Drug down the blindfold sense of wrong
That so my pleasure may be whole;

While now we talk as once we talk'd
　　Of men and minds, the dust of change,
　　The days that grow to something strange,
In walking as of old we walk'd

Beside the river's wooded reach,
　　The fortress, and the mountain ridge,
　　The cataract flashing from the bridge,
The breaker breaking on the beach.

LXXI.

Risest thou thus, dim dawn, again,
 And howlest, issuing out of night,
 With blasts that blow the poplar white,
And lash with storm the streaming pane?

Day, when my crown'd estate begun
 To pine in that reverse of doom,
 Which sicken'd every living bloom,
And blurr'd the splendour of the sun;

Who usherest in the dolorous hour
 With thy quick tears that make the rose
 Pull sideways, and the daisy close
Her crimson fringes to the shower;

Who might'st have heaved a windless flame
 Up the deep East, or, whispering, play'd
 A chequer-work of beam and shade
Along the hills, yet look'd the same,

As wan, as chill, as wild as now;
 Day, mark'd as with some hideous crime,
 When the dark hand struck down thro' time,
And cancell'd nature's best: but thou,

Lift as thou may'st thy burthen'd brows
  Thro' clouds that drench the morning star,
  And whirl the ungarner'd sheaf afar,
And sow the sky with flying boughs,

And up thy vault with roaring sound
  Climb thy thick noon, disastrous day;
  Touch thy dull goal of joyless gray,
And hide thy shame beneath the ground.

LXIII.

So many worlds, so much to do,
    So little done, such things to be,
    How know I what had need of thee,
For thou wert strong as thou wert true?

The fame is quench'd that I foresaw,
    The head hath miss'd an earthly wreath:
    I curse not nature, no, nor death;
For nothing is that errs from law.

We pass; the path that each man trod
    Is dim, or will be dim, with weeds:
    What fame is left for human deeds
In endless age? It rests with God.

O hollow wraith of dying fame,
    Fade wholly, while the soul exults,
    And self-infolds the large results
Of force that would have forged a name.

LXXIII.

As sometimes in a dead man's face,
    To those that watch it more and more,
    A likeness, hardly seen before,
Comes out — to some one of his race:

So, dearest, now thy brows are cold,
    I see thee what thou art, and know
    Thy likeness to the wise below,
Thy kindred with the great of old.

But there is more than I can see,
    And what I see I leave unsaid,
    Nor speak it, knowing Death has made
His darkness beautiful with thee.

LXXIV.

I LEAVE thy praises unexpress'd
    In verse that brings myself relief,
    And by the measure of my grief
I leave thy greatness to be guess'd;

What practice howsoe'er expert
    In fitting aptest words to things,
    Or voice the richest-toned that sings,
Hath power to give thee as thou wert?

I care not in these fading days
    To raise a cry that lasts not long,
    And round thee with the breeze of song
To stir a little dust of praise.

Thy leaf has perish'd in the green,
    And, while we breathe beneath the sun,
    The world which credits what is done
Is cold to all that might have been.

So here shall silence guard thy fame;
    But somewhere, out of human view,
    Whate'er thy hands are set to do
Is wrought with tumult of acclaim.

LXXV.

Take wings of fancy, and ascend,
    And in a moment set thy face
    Where all the starry heavens of space
Are sharpen'd to a needle's end;

Take wings of foresight; lighten thro'
    The secular abyss to come,
    And lo, thy deepest lays are dumb
Before the mouldering of a yew;

And if the matin songs, that woke
    The darkness of our planet, last,
    Thine own shall wither in the vast,
Ere half the lifetime of an oak.

Ere these have clothed their branchy bowers
    With fifty Mays, thy songs are vain;
    And what are they when these remain
The ruin'd shells of hollow towers?

LXXVI.

What hope is here for modern rhyme
　　To him, who turns a musing eye
　　On songs, and deeds, and lives, that lie
Foreshorten'd in the tract of time?

These mortal lullabies of pain
　　May bind a book, may line a box,
　　May serve to curl a maiden's locks;
Or when a thousand moons shall wane

A man upon a stall may find,
　　And, passing, turn the page that tells
　　A grief, then changed to something else,
Sung by a long-forgotten mind.

But what of that? My darken'd ways –
　　Shall ring with music all the same;
　　To breathe my loss is more than fame,
To utter love more sweet than praise.

Again at Christmas did we weave
      The holly round the Christmas hearth;
      The silent snow possess'd the earth,
And calmly fell our Christmas-eve:

The yule-clog sparkled keen with frost,
      No wing of wind the region swept,
      But over all things brooding slept
The quiet sense of something lost.

As in the winters left behind,
      Again our ancient games had place,
      The mimic picture's breathing grace,
And dance and song and hoodman-blind.

Who show'd a token of distress?
      No single tear, no mark of pain:
      O sorrow, then can sorrow wane?
O grief, can grief be changed to less?

O last regret, regret can die!
      No — mixt with all this mystic frame,
      Her deep relations are the same,
But with long use her tears are dry.

LXXVIII.

"More than my brothers are to me" —
    Let this not vex thee, noble heart!
    I know thee of what force thou art
To hold the costliest love in fee.

But thou and I are one in kind,
    As moulded like in nature's mint;
    And hill and wood and field did print
The same sweet forms in either mind.

For us the same cold streamlet curl'd
    Thro' all his eddying coves; the same
    All winds that roam the twilight came
In whispers of the beauteous world.

At one dear knee we proffer'd vows,
    One lesson from one book we learn'd,
    Ere childhood's flaxen ringlet turn'd
To black and brown on kindred brows.

And so my wealth resembles thine,
    But he was rich where I was poor,
    And he supplied my want the more
As his unlikeness fitted mine.

LXXI.

If any vague desire should rise,
    That holy Death ere Arthur died
    Had moved me kindly from his side,
And dropt the dust on tearless eyes;

Then fancy shapes, as fancy can,
    The grief my loss in him had wrought,
    A grief as deep as life or thought,
But stay'd in peace with God and man.

I make a picture in the brain;
    I hear the sentence that he speaks;
    He bears the burthen of the weeks,
But turns his burthen into gain.

His credit thus shall set me free;
    And, influence-rich to soothe and save,
    Unused example from the grave
Reach out dead hands to comfort me.

LXXX.

Could I have said while he was here
    "My love shall now no further range;
    There cannot come a mellower change,
For now is love mature in ear."

Love, then, had hope of richer store:
    What end is here to my complaint?
    This haunting whisper makes me faint,
"More years had made me love thee more."

But Death returns an answer sweet:
    "My sudden frost was sudden gain,
    And gave all ripeness to the grain,
It might have drawn from after-heat."

LXXXI.

I WAGE not any feud with Death
    For changes wrought on form and face;
    No lower life that earth's embrace
May breed with him, can fright my faith.

Eternal process moving on,
    From state to state the spirit walks;
    And these are but the shatter'd stalks,
Or ruin'd chrysalis of one.

Nor blame I Death, because he bare
    The use of virtue out of earth:
    I know transplanted human worth
Will bloom to profit, otherwhere.

For this alone on Death I wreak
    The wrath that garners in my heart;
    He put our lives so far apart
We cannot hear each other speak.

LXXXII.

Dip down upon the northern shore,
    O sweet new-year delaying long;
    Thou doest expectant nature wrong;
Delaying long, delay no more.

What stays thee from the clouded noons,
    Thy sweetness from its proper place?
    Can trouble live with April days,
Or sadness in the summer moons?

Bring orchis, bring the foxglove spire,
    The little speedwell's darling blue,
    Deep tulips dash'd with fiery dew,
Laburnums, dropping-wells of fire.

O thou, new-year, delaying long,
    Delayest the sorrow in my blood,
    That longs to burst a frozen bud,
And flood a fresher throat with song.

LXXXIII.

When I contemplate all alone
    The life that had been thine below,
    And fix my thoughts on all the glow
To which thy crescent would have grown;

I see thee sitting crown'd with good,
    A central warmth diffusing bliss
    In glance and smile, and clasp and kiss,
On all the branches of thy blood;

Thy blood, my friend, and partly mine;
    For now the day was drawing on,
    When thou should'st link thy life with one
Of mine own house, and boys of thine

Had babbled "Uncle" on my knee;
    But that remorseless iron hour
    Made cypress of her orange flower,
Despair of Hope, and earth of thee.

I seem to meet their least desire,
    To clap their cheeks, to call them mine.
    I see their unborn faces shine
Beside the never-lighted fire.

I see myself an honour'd guest,
    Thy partner in the flowery walk
    Of letters, genial table-talk,
Or deep dispute, and graceful jest,

While now thy prosperous labour fills
    The lips of men with honest praise,
    And sun by sun the happy days
Descend below the golden hills

With promise of a morn as fair;
    And all the train of bounteous hours
    Conduct by paths of growing powers,
To reverence and the silver hair;

Till slowly worn her earthly robe,
    Her lavish mission richly wrought,
    Leaving great legacies of thought,
Thy spirit should fail from off the' globe;

What time mine own might also flee,
    As link'd with thine in love and fate,
    And, hovering o'er the dolorous strait
To the other shore, involved in thee,

Arrive at last the blessed goal,
    And He that died in Holy Land
    Would reach us out the shining hand,
And take us as a single soul.

What reed was that on which I leant?
    Ah, backward fancy, wherefore wake
    The old bitterness again, and break
The low beginnings of content.

LXXXIV.

This truth came borne with bier and pall,
 I felt it, when I sorrow'd most,
 'Tis better to have loved and lost,
Than never to have loved at all ——

O true in word, and tried in deed,
 Demanding, so to bring relief
 To this which is our common grief,
What kind of life is that I lead;

And whether trust in things above
 Be dimm'd of sorrow, or sustain'd;
 And whether love for him have drain'd
My capabilities of love;

Your words have virtue such as draws
 A faithful answer from the breast,
 'Thro' light reproaches, half exprest,
And loyal unto kindly laws.

My blood an even tenor kept,
 Till on mine ear this message falls,
 That in Vienna's fatal walls
God's finger touch'd him, and he slept.

The great Intelligences fair
 That range above our mortal state,
 In circle round the blessed gate,
Received and gave him welcome there;

And led him thro' the blissful climes,
    And show'd him in the fountain fresh
    All knowledge that the sons of flesh
Shall gather in the cycled times.

But I remain'd, whose hopes were dim,
    Whose life, whose thoughts were little worth,
    To wander on a darken'd earth,
Where all things round me breathed of him.

O friendship, equal-poised control,
    O heart, with kindliest motion warm,
    O sacred essence, other form,
O solemn ghost, O crowned soul!

Yet none could better know than I,
    How much of act at human hands
    The sense of human will demands,
By which we dare to live or die.

Whatever way my days decline,
    I felt and feel, tho' left alone,
    His being working in mine own,
The footsteps of his life in mine;

A life that all the Muses deck'd
    With gifts of grace, that might express
    All-comprehensive tenderness,
All subtilising intellect:

7*.

And so my passion hath not swerved
    To works of weakness, but I find
    An image comforting the mind,
And in my grief a strength reserved.

Likewise the imaginative woe,
    That loved to handle spiritual strife,
    Diffused the shock thro' all my life,
But in the present broke the blow.

My pulses therefore beat again
    For other friends that once I met;
    Nor can it suit me to forget
The mighty hopes that make us men.

I woo your love: I count it crime
    To mourn for any overmuch;
    I, the divided half of such
A friendship as had master'd Time;

Which masters Time indeed, and is
    Eternal, separate from fears:
    The all-assuming months and years
Can take no part away from this:

But Summer on the steaming floods,
    And Spring that swells the narrow brooks,
    And Autumn, with a noise of rooks,
That gather in the waning woods,

And every pulse of wind and wave
    Recalls, in change of light or gloom,
    My old affection of the tomb,
And my prime passion in the grave:

My old affection of the tomb,
    A part of stillness, yearns to speak:
    "Arise, and get thee forth and seek
A friendship for the years to come.

I watch thee from the quiet shore;
    Thy spirit up to mine can reach;
    But in dear words of human speech
We two communicate no more."

And I, "Can clouds of nature stain
    The starry clearness of the free?
    How is it? Canst thou feel for me
Some painless sympathy with pain?"

And lightly does the whisper fall;
    "'Tis hard for thee to fathom this;
    I triumph in conclusive bliss,
And that serene result of all."

So hold I commerce with the dead;
    Or so methinks the dead would say;
    Or so shall grief with symbols play,
And pining life be fancy-fed.

Now looking to some settled end,
    That these things pass, and I shall prove
    A meeting somewhere, love with love,
I crave your pardon, O my friend;

If not so fresh, with love as true,
    I, clasping brother-hands, aver
    I could not, if I would, transfer
The whole I felt for him to you.

For which be they that hold apart
    The promise of the golden hours?
    First love, first friendship, equal powers,
That marry with the virgin heart.

Still mine, that cannot but deplore,
    That beats within a lonely place,
    That yet remembers his embrace,
But at his footstep leaps no more.

My heart, tho' widow'd, may not rest
    Quite in the love of what is gone,
    But seeks to beat in time with one
That warms another living breast.

Ah, take the imperfect gift I bring,
    Knowing the primrose yet is dear,
    Tho primrose of the later year,
As not unlike to that of Spring.

LXXXV.

Sweet after showers, ambrosial air,
      That rollest from the gorgeous gloom
      Of evening over brake and bloom
And meadow, slowly breathing bare

The round of space, and rapt below
      Thro' all the dewy-tassell'd wood,
      And shadowing down the horned flood
In ripples, fan my brows and blow

The fever from my cheek, and sigh
      The full new life that feeds thy breath
      Throughout my frame, till Doubt and Death,
Ill brethren, let the fancy fly

From belt to belt of crimson seas
      On leagues of odour streaming far,
      To where in yonder orient star
A hundred spirits whisper "Peace."

LXXXVI.

I PAST beside the reverend walls
    In which of old I wore the gown;
    I roved at random thro' the town,
And saw the tumult of the halls;

And heard once more in college fanes
    The storm their high-built organs make,
    And thunder-music, rolling, shake
The prophets blazon'd on the panes;

And caught once more the distant shout,
    The measured pulse of racing oars
    Among the willows; paced the shores
And many a bridge, and all about

The same gray flats again, and felt
    The same, but not the same; and last
    Up that long walk of limes I past
To see the rooms in which he dwelt.

Another name was on the door:
    I linger'd; all within was noise
    Of songs, and clapping hands, and boys
That crash'd the glass and beat the floor;

Where once we held debate, a band
　　Of youthful friends, on mind and art,
　　And labour, and the changing mart,
And all the framework of the land;

When one would aim an arrow fair,
　　But send it slackly from the string;
　　And one would pierce an outer ring,
And one an inner, here and there;

And last the master-bowman, he,
　　Would cleave the mark.　A willing ear
　　We lent him.　Who, but hung to hear
The rapt oration flowing free

From point to point, with power and grace
　　And music in the bounds of law,
　　To those conclusions when we saw
The God within him light his face,

And seem to lift the form, and glow
　　In azure orbits heavenly-wise;
　　And over those ethereal eyes
The bar of Michael Angelo.

LXXXVII.

WILD bird, whose warble, liquid sweet,
　　Rings Eden thro' the budded quicks,
　　O tell me where the senses mix,
O tell me where the passions meet,

Whence radiate: fierce extremes employ
　　Thy spirits in the darkening leaf,
　　And in the midmost heart of grief
Thy passion clasps a secret joy:

And I — my harp would prelude woe —
　　I cannot all command the strings;
　　The glory of the sum of things
Will flash along the chords and go.

LXXXVIII.

WITCH-ELMS that counterchange the floor
    Of this flat lawn with dusk and bright;
    And thou, with all thy breadth and height
Of foliage, towering sycamore;

How often, hither wandering down,
    My Arthur found your shadows fair,
    And shook to all the liberal air
The dust and din and steam of town:

He brought an eye for all he saw;
    He mixt in all our simple sports;
    They pleased him, fresh from brawling courts
And dusty purlieus of the law.

O joy to him in this retreat,
    Immantled in ambrosial dark,
    To drink the cooler air, and mark
The landscape winking thro' the heat:

O sound to rout the brood of cares,
    The sweep of scythe in morning dew,
    The gust that round the garden flew,
And tumbled half the mellowing pears!

O bliss, when all in circle drawn
    About him, heart and ear were fed
    To hear him, as he lay and read
The Tuscan poets on the lawn:

Or in the all-golden afternoon
    A guest, or happy sister, sung,
    Or here she brought the harp and flung
A ballad to the brightening moon:

Nor less it pleased in livelier moods,
    Beyond the bounding hill to stray,
    And break the livelong summer day
With banquet in the distant woods;

Whereat we glanced from theme to theme,
    Discuss'd the books to love or hate,
    Or touch'd the changes of the state,
Or threaded some Socratic dream;

But if I praised the busy town,
    He loved to rail against it still,
    For "ground in yonder social mill
We rub each other's angles down,

And merge" he said "in form and gloss
    The picturesque of man and man."
    We talk'd: the stream beneath us ran,
The wine-flask lying couch'd in moss,

Or cool'd within the glooming wave;
    And last, returning from afar,
    Before the crimson-circled star
Had fall'n into her father's grave,

And brushing ankle-deep in flowers,
    We heard behind the woodbine veil
    The milk that bubbled in the pail,
And buzzings of the honied hours.

LXXXIX.

He tasted love with half his mind,
  Nor ever drank the inviolate spring
  Where nighest heaven, who first could fling
This bitter seed among mankind;

That could the dead, whose dying eyes
  Were closed with wail, resume their life,
  They would but find in child and wife
An iron welcome when they rise:

'Twas well, indeed, when warm with wine,
  To pledge them with a kindly tear,
  To talk them o'er, to wish them here,
To count their memories half divine;

But if they came who past away,
  Behold their brides in other hands;
  The hard heir strides about their lands,
And will not yield them for a day.

Yea, tho' their sons were none of these,
  Not less the yet-loved sire would make
  Confusion worse than death, and shake
The pillars of domestic peace.

Ah dear, but come thou back to me:
  Whatever change the years have wrought,
  I find not yet one lonely thought
That cries against my wish for thee.

XC.

When rosy plumelets tuft the larch,
      And rarely pipes the mounted thrush;
      Or underneath the barren bush
Flits by the sea-blue bird of March;

Come, wear the form by which I know
      Thy spirit in time among thy peers;
      The hope of unaccomplish'd years
Be large and lucid round thy brow.

When summer's hourly-mellowing change
      May breathe, with many roses sweet,
      Upon the thousand waves of wheat,
That ripple round the lonely grange;

Come: not in watches of the night,
      But where the sunbeam broodeth warm,
      Come, beauteous in thine after form,
And like a finer light in light.

XCI.

If any vision should reveal
    Thy likeness, I might count it vain
    As but the canker of the brain;
Yea, tho' it spake and made appeal

To chances where our lots were cast
    Together in the days behind,
    I might but say, I hear a wind
Of memory murmuring the past.

Yea, tho' it spake and bared to view
    A fact within the coming year;
    And tho' the months, revolving near,
Should prove the phantom-warning true,

They might not seem thy prophecies,
    But spiritual presentiments,
    And such refraction of events
As often rises ere they rise.

XCII.

I SHALL not see thee.   Dare I say
      No spirit ever brake the band
      That stays him from the native land,
Where first he walk'd when claspt in clay?

No visual shade of some one lost,
      But he, the Spirit himself, may come
      Where all the nerve of sense is numb;
Spirit to Spirit, Ghost to Ghost.

O, therefore from thy sightless range
      With gods in unconjectured bliss,
      O, from the distance of the abyss
Of tenfold-complicated change,

Descend, and touch, and enter; hear
      The wish too strong for words to name;
      That in this blindness of the frame
My Ghost may feel that thine is near.

XCIII.

How pure at heart and sound in head,
    With what divine affections bold
    Should be the man whose thought would hold
An hour's communion with the dead.

In vain shalt thou, or any, call
    The spirits from their golden day,
    Except, like them, thou too canst say,
My spirit is at peace with all.

They haunt the silence of the breast,
    Imaginations calm and fair,
    The memory like a cloudless air,
The conscience as a sea at rest:

But when the heart is full of din,
    And doubt beside the portal waits,
    They can but listen at the gates,
And hear the household jar within.

XCIV.

By night we linger'd on the lawn,
    For underfoot the herb was dry;
    And genial warmth; and o'er the sky
The silvery haze of summer drawn;

And calm that let the tapers burn
    Unwavering: not a cricket chirr'd:
    The brook alone far-off was heard,
And on the board the fluttering urn:

And bats went round in fragrant skies,
    And wheel'd or lit the filmy shapes
    That haunt the dusk, with ermine capes
And woolly breasts and beaded eyes;

While now we sang old songs that peal'd
    From knoll to knoll, where, couch'd at ease,
    The white kine glimmer'd, and the trees
Laid their dark arms about the field.

But when those others, one by one,
    Withdrew themselves from me and night,
    And in the house light after light
Went out, and I was all alone,

8*

A hunger seized my heart; I read
    Of that glad year which once had been,
    In those fall'n leaves which kept their green,
The noble letters of the dead:

And strangely on the silence broke
    The silent-speaking words, and strange
    Was love's dumb cry defying change
To test his worth; and strangely spoke

The faith, the vigour, bold to dwell
    On doubts that drive the coward back,
    And keen thro' wordy snares to track
Suggestion to her inmost cell.

So word by word, and line by line,
    The dead man touch'd me from the past,
    And all at once it seem'd at last
His living soul was flash'd on mine,

And mine in his was wound, and whirl'd
    About empyreal heights of thought,
    And came on that which is, and caught
The deep pulsations of the world,

Æonian music measuring out
    The steps of Time — the shocks of Chance —
    The blows of Death.   At length my trance
Was cancell'd, stricken thro' with doubt.

Vague words! but ah, how hard to frame
    In matter-moulded forms of speech,
    Or ev'n for intellect to reach
Thro' memory that which I became:

'Till now the doubtful dusk reveal'd
    The knolls once more where, couch'd at ease,
    The white kine glimmer'd, and the trees
Laid their dark arms about the field:

And suck'd from out the distant gloom
    A breeze began to tremble o'er
    The large leaves of the sycamore,
  And fluctuate all the still perfume,

And gathering freshlier overhead,
    Rock'd the full-foliaged elms, and swung
    The heavy-folded rose, and flung
The lilies to and fro, and said

"The dawn, the dawn," and died away;
    And East and West, without a breath,
    Mixt their dim lights, like life and death,
To broaden into boundless day.

XCV.

You say, but with no touch of scorn,
  Sweet-hearted, you, whose light-blue eyes
  Are tender over drowning flies,
You tell me, doubt is Devil-born.

I know not: one indeed I know
  In many a subtle question versed,
  Who touch'd a jarring lyre at first,
But ever strove to make it true:

Perplext in faith, but pure in deeds,
  At last he beat his music out.
  There lives more faith in honest doubt,
Believe me, than in half the creeds.

He fought his doubts and gather'd strength,
  He would not make his judgement blind,
  He faced the spectres of the mind
And laid them: thus he came at length

To find a stronger faith his own;
  And Power was with him in the night,
  Which makes the darkness and the light,
And dwells not in the light alone,

But in the darkness and the cloud,
  As over Sinai's peaks of old,
  While Israel made their gods of gold,
Altho' the trumpet blew so loud.

XCVI.

My love has talk'd with rocks and trees;
    He finds on misty mountain-grouud
    His own vast shadow glory-crown'd;
He sees himself in all he sees.

Two partners of a married life —
    I look'd on these and thought of thee
    In vastness and in mystery,
And of my spirit as of a wife.

These two — they dwelt with eye on eye,
    Their hearts of old have beat in tune,
    Their meetings made December June,
Their every parting was to die.

Their love has never past away;
    The days she never can forget
    Are earnest that he loves her yet,
Whate'er the faithless people say.

Her life is lone, he sits apart,
    He loves her yet, she will not weep,
    Tho' rapt in matters dark and deep
He seems to slight her simple heart.

He thrids the labyrinth of the mind,
    He reads the secret of the star,
    He seems so near and yet so far,
He looks so cold: she thinks him kind.

She keeps the gift of years before,
    A wither'd violet is her bliss;
    She knows not what his greatness is;
For that, for all, she loves him more.

For him she plays, to him she sings
    Of early faith and plighted vows;
    She knows but matters of the house,
And he, he knows a thousand things.

Her faith is fixt and cannot move,
    She darkly feels him great and wise,
    She dwells on him with faithful eyes,
"I cannot understand: I love."

XCVII.

You leave us: you will see the Rhine,
    And those fair hills I sail'd below,
    When I was there with him; and go
By summer belts of wheat and vine

To where he breathed his latest breath,
    That City. All her splendour seems
    No livelier than the wisp that gleams
On Lethe in the eyes of Death.

Let her great Danube rolling fair
    Enwind her isles, unmark'd of me:
    I have not seen, I will not see
Vienna; rather dream that there,

A treble darkness, Evil haunts
    The birth, the bridal; friend from friend
    Is oftener parted, fathers bend
Above more graves, a thousand wants

Gnarr at the heels of men, and prey
    By each cold hearth, and sadness flings
    Her shadow on the blaze of kings:
And yet myself have heard him say,

That not in any mother town
  With statelier progress to and fro
  The double tides of chariots flow
By park and suburb under brown

Of lustier leaves; nor more content,
  He told me, lives in any crowd,
  When all is gay with lamps, and loud
With sport and song, in booth and tent,

Imperial halls, or open plain;
  And wheels the circled dance, and breaks
  The rocket molten into flakes
Of crimson or in emerald rain.

XCVIII.

RISEST thou thus, dim dawn, again,
　　So loud with voices of the birds,
　　So thick with lowings of the herds,
Day, when I lost the flower of men;

Who tremblest thro' thy darkling red
　　On yon swoll'n brook that bubbles fast
　　By meadows breathing of the past,
And woodlands holy to the dead;

Who murmurest in the foliaged caves
　　A song that slights the coming care,
　　And Autumn laying here and there
A fiery finger on the leaves;

Who wakenest with thy balmy breath
　　To myriads on the genial earth,
　　Memories of bridal, or of birth,
And unto myriads more, of death.

O, wheresoever those may be,
　　Betwixt the slumber of the poles,
　　To-day they count as kindred souls;
They know me not, but mourn with me.

XCIX.

I CLIMB the hill: from end to end
    Of all the landscape underneath,
    I find no place that does not breathe
Some gracious memory of my friend;

No gray old grange, or lonely fold,
    Or low morass and whispering reed,
    Or simple stile from mead to mead,
Or sheepwalk up the windy wold;

Nor hoary knoll of ash and haw
    That hears the latest linnet trill,
    Nor quarry trench'd along the hill,
And haunted by the wrangling daw;

Nor runlet tinkling from the rock;
    Nor pastoral rivulet that swerves
    To left and right thro' meadowy curves,
That feed the mothers of the flock;

But each has pleased a kindred eye,
    And each reflects a kindlier day;
    And, leaving these, to pass away,
I think once more he seems to die.

O.

Unwatch'd, the garden bough shall sway,
    The tender blossom flutter down,
    Unloved, that beech will gather brown,
This maple burn itself away;

Unloved, the sun-flower, shining fair,
    Ray round with flames her disk of seed,
    And many a rose-carnation feed
With summer spice the humming air;

Unloved, by many a sandy bar,
    The brook shall babble down the plain,
    At noon or when the lesser wain
Is twisting round the polar star;

Uncared for, gird the windy grove,
    And flood the haunts of hern and crake;
    Or into silver arrows break
The sailing moon in creek and cove;

Till from the garden and the wild
    A fresh association blow,
    And year by year the landscape grow
Familiar to the stranger's child;

As year by year the labourer tills
    His wonted glebe, or lops the glades;
    And year by year our memory fades
From all the circle of the hills.

CI.

We leave the well-beloved place
  Where first we gazed upon the sky;
  The roofs, that heard our earliest cry,
Will shelter one of stranger race.

We go, but ere we go from home,
  As down the garden-walks I move,
  Two spirits of a diverse love
Contend for loving masterdom.

One whispers, here thy boyhood sung
  Long since its matin song, and heard
  The low love-language of the bird
In native hazels tassel-hung.

The other answers, "Yea, but here
  Thy feet have stray'd in after hours
  With thy lost friend among the bowers,
And this hath made them trebly dear."

These two have striven half the day,
  And each prefers his separate claim,
  Poor rivals in a losing game,
That will not yield each other way.

I turn to go: my feet are set
  To leave the pleasant fields and farms;
  They mix in one another's arms
To one pure image of regret.

CII.

On that last night before we went
    From out the doors where I was bred,
    I dream'd a vision of the dead,
Which left my after-morn content.

Methought I dwelt within a hall,
    And maidens with me: distant hills
    From hidden summits fed with rills
A river sliding by the wall.

The hall with harp and carol rang.
    They sang of what is wise and good
    And graceful.   In the centre stood
A statue veil'd, to which they sang;

And which, tho' veil'd, was known to me,
    The shape of him I loved, and love
    For ever: then flew in a dove
And brought a summons from the sea:

And when they learnt that I must go
    They wept and wail'd, but led the way
    To where a little shallop lay
At anchor in the flood below;

And on by many a level mead,
    And shadowing bluff that made the banks,
    We glided winding under ranks
Of iris, and the golden reed;

And still as vaster grew the shore,
    And roll'd the floods in grander space,
    The maidens gather'd strength and grace
And presence, lordlier than before;

And I myself, who sat apart
    And watch'd them, wax'd in every limb;
    I felt the thews of Anakim,
The pulses of a Titan's heart;

As one would sing the death of war,
    And one would chant the history
    Of that great race, which is to be,
And one the shaping of a star;

Until the forward-creeping tides
    Began to foam, and we to draw
    From deep to deep, to where we saw
A great ship lift her shining sides.

The man we loved was there on deck,
    But thrice as large as man he bent
    To greet us.   Up the side I went,
And fell in silence on his neck:

Whereat those maidens with one mind
      Bewail'd their lot; I did them wrong:
      "We served thee here," they said, "so long,
And wilt thou leave us now behind?"

So rapt I was, they could not win
      An answer from my lips, but he
      Replying, "Enter likewise ye
And go with us:" they enter'd in.

And while the wind began to sweep
      A music out of sheet and shroud,
      We steer'd her toward a crimson cloud
That landlike slept along the deep.

CIII.

The time draws near the birth of Christ;
    The moon is hid, the night is still;
    A single church below the hill
Is pealing, folded in the mist.

A single peal of bells below,
    That wakens at this hour of rest
    A single murmur in the breast,
That these are not the bells I know.

Like strangers' voices here they sound,
    In lands where not a memory strays,
    Nor landmark breathes of other days,
But all is new unhallow'd ground.

CIV.

Tins holly by the cottage-eave,
    To-night, ungather'd, shall it stand:
    We live within the stranger's land,
And strangely falls our Christmas eve.

Our father's dust is left alone
    And silent under other snows:
    There in due time the woodbine blows,
The violet comes, but we are gone.

No more shall wayward grief abuse
    The genial hour with mask and mime;
    For change of place, like growth of time,
Has broke the bond of dying use.

Let cares that petty shadows cast,
    By which our lives are chiefly proved,
    A little spare the night I loved,
And hold it solemn to the past.

But let no footstep beat the floor,
    Nor bowl of wassail mantle warm;
    For who would keep an ancient form
Thro' which the spirit breathes no more?

Be neither song, nor game, nor feast;
    Nor harp be touch'd, nor flute be blown;
    No dance, no motion, save alone
What lightens in the lucid east

Of rising worlds by yonder wood.
    Long sleeps the summer in the seed;
    Run out your measured arcs, and lead
The closing cycle rich in good.

CV.

Ring out wild bells to the wild sky,
 The flying cloud, the frosty light:
 The year is dying in the night;
Ring out, wild bells, and let him die.

Ring out the old, ring in the new,
 Ring, happy bells, across the snow:
 The year is going, let him go;
Ring out the false, ring in the true.

Ring out the grief that saps the mind,
 For those that here we see no more;
 Ring out the feud of rich and poor,
Ring in redress to all mankind.

Ring out a slowly dying cause,
 And ancient forms of party strife;
 Ring in the nobler modes of life,
With sweeter manners, purer laws.

Ring out the want, the care, the sin,
 The faithless coldness of the times;
 Ring out, ring out my mournful rhymes,
But ring the fuller minstrel in.

Ring out false pride in place and blood,
    The civic slander and the spite;
    Ring in the love of truth and right, .
Ring in the common love of good.

Ring out old shapes of foul disease;
    Ring out the narrowing lust of gold;
    Ring out the thousand wars of old,
Ring in the thousand years of peace.

Ring in the valiant man and free,
    The larger heart, the kindlier hand;
    Ring out the darkness of the land,
Ring in the Christ that is to be.

CVI.

It is the day when he was born,
    A bitter day that early sank
    Behind a purple-frosty bank
Of vapour, leaving night forlorn.

The time admits not flowers or leaves
    To deck the banquet. Fiercely flies
    The blast of North and East, and ice
Makes daggers at the sharpen'd eaves,

And bristles all the brakes and thorns
    To yon hard crescent, as she hangs
    Above the wood which grides and clangs
Its leafless ribs and iron horns

Together, in the drifts that pass
    To darken on the rolling brine
    That breaks the coast. But fetch the wine,
Arrange the board and brim the glass;

Bring in great logs and let them lie,
    To make a solid core of heat;
    Be cheerful-minded, talk and treat
Of all things ev'n as he were by;

We keep the day. With festal cheer,
    With books and music, surely we
    Will drink to him whate'er he be,
And sing the songs he loved to hear.

CVII.

I WILL not shut me from my kind,
    And, lest I stiffen into stone,
    I will not eat my heart alone,
Nor feed with sighs a passing wind:

What profit lies in barren faith,
    And vacant yearning, tho' with might
    To scale the heaven's highest height,
Or dive below the wells of Death?

What find I in the highest place,
    But mine own phantom chanting hymns?
    And on the depths of death there swims
The reflex of a human face.

I'll rather take what fruit may be
    Of sorrow under human skies:
    'Tis held that sorrow makes us wise,
Whatever wisdom sleep with thee.

CVIII.

Heart-affluence in discursive talk
      From household fountains never dry;
      The critic clearness of an eye,
That saw thro' all the Muses' walk;

Seraphic intellect and force
      To seize and throw the doubts of man;
      Impassion'd logic, which outran
The hearer in its fiery course;

High nature amorous of the good,
      But touch'd with no ascetic gloom;
      And passion pure in snowy bloom
Thro' all the years of April blood;

A love of freedom rarely felt,
      Of freedom in her regal seat
      Of England; not the schoolboy heat,
The blind hysterics of the Celt;

And manhood fused with female grace
      In such a sort, the child would twine
      A trustful hand, unask'd, in thine,
And find his comfort in thy face;

All these have been, and thee mine eyes
      Have look'd on: if they look'd in vain,
      My shame is greater who remain,
Nor let thy wisdom make me wise.

CIX.

Thy converse drew us with delight,
　　The men of rathe and riper years:
　　The feeble soul, a haunt of fears,
Forgot his weakness in thy sight.

On thee the loyal-hearted hung,
　　The proud was half disarm'd of pride,
　　Nor cared the serpent at thy side
To flicker with his double tongue.

The stern were mild when thou wert by,
　　The flippant put himself to school
　　And heard thee, and the brazen fool
Was soften'd, and he knew not why;

While I, thy dearest, sat apart,
　　And felt thy triumph was as mine;
　　And loved them more, that they were thine,
The graceful tact, the Christian art;

Not mine the sweetness or the skill,
　　But mine the love that will not tire,
　　And, born of love, the vague desire
That spurs an imitative will.

CX.

The churl in spirit, up or down
    Along the scale of ranks, thro' all,
    To him who grasps a golden ball,
By blood a king, at heart a clown;

The churl in spirit, howe'er he veil
    His want in forms for fashion's sake,
    Will let his coltish nature break
At seasons thro' the gilded pale:

For who can always act? but he,
    To whom a thousand memories call,
    Not being less but more than all
The gentleness he seem'd to be,

Best seem'd the thing he was, and join'd
    Each office of the social hour
    To noble manners, as the flower
And native growth of noble mind;

Nor ever narrowness or spite,
    Or villain fancy fleeting by,
    Drew in the expression of an eye,
Where God and Nature met in light;

And thus he bore without abuse
    The grand old name of gentleman,
    Defamed by every charlatan,
And soil'd with all ignoble use.

CXI.

High wisdom holds my wisdom less,
    That I, who gaze with temperate eyes
    On glorious insufficiencies,
Set light by narrower perfectness.

But thou, that fillest all the room
    Of all my love, art reason why
    I seem to cast a careless eye
On souls, the lesser lords of doom.

For what wert thou? some novel power
    Sprang up for ever at a touch,
    And hope could never hope too much,
In watching thee from hour to hour,

Large elements in order brought,
    And tracts of calm from tempest made,
    And world-wide fluctuation sway'd
In vassal tides that follow'd thought.

CIII.

'Tis held that sorrow makes us wise;
    Yet how much wisdom sleeps with thee
    Which not alone had guided me,
But served the seasons that may rise;

For can I doubt who knew thee keen
    In intellect, with force and skill
    To strive, to fashion, to fulfil —
I doubt not what thou wouldst have been:

A life in civic action warm,
    A soul on highest mission sent,
    A potent voice of Parliament,
A pillar steadfast in the storm,

Should licensed boldness gather force,
    Becoming, when the time has birth,
    A lever to uplift the earth
And roll it in another course,

With thousand shocks that come and go,
    With agonies, with energies,
    With overthrowings, and with cries,
And undulations to and fro.

CXIII.

Who loves not Knowledge? Who shall rail
    Against her beauty? May she mix
    With men and prosper! Who shall fix
Her pillars? Let her work prevail.

But on her forehead sits a fire:
    She sets her forward countenance
    And leaps into the future chance,
Submitting all things to desire.

Half-grown as yet, a child, and vain—
    She cannot fight the fear of death.
    What is she, cut from love and faith,
But some wild Pallas from the brain

Of Demons? fiery-hot to burst
    All barriers in her onward race
    For power. Let her know her place;
She is the second, not the first.

A higher hand must make her mild,
    If all be not in vain; and guide
    Her footsteps, moving side by side
With wisdom, like the younger child:

For she is earthly of the mind,
    But Wisdom heavenly of the soul.
    O, friend, who camest to thy goal
So early, leaving me behind,

I would the great world grow like thee,
    Who growest not alone in power
    And knowledge, but by year and hour
In reverence and in charity.

CXIV.

Now fades the last long streak of snow,
    Now burgeons every maze of quick
    About the flowering squares, and thick
By ashen roots the violets blow.

Now rings the woodland loud and long.
    The distance takes a lovelier hue,
    And drown'd in yonder living blue
The lark becomes a sightless song.

Now dance the lights on lawn and lea,
    The flocks are whiter down the vale,
    And milkier every milky sail
On winding stream or distant sea;

Where now the seamew pipes, or dives
    In yonder greening gleam, and fly
    The happy birds, that change their sky
To build and brood; that live their lives

From land to land; and in my breast
    Spring wakens too; and my regret
    Becomes an April violet, –
And buds and blossoms like the rest.

CXV.

Is it, then, regret for buried time
    That keenlier in sweet April wakes,
    And meets the year, and gives and takes
The colours of the crescent prime?

Not all: the songs, the stirring air,
    The life re-orient out of dust,
    Cry thro' the sense to hearten trust
In that which made the world so fair.

Not all regret: the face will shine
    Upon me, while I muse alone;
    And that dear voice, I once have known,
Still speak to me of me and mine:

Yet less of sorrow lives in me
    For days of happy commune dead;
    Less yearning for the friendship fled,
Than some strong bond which is to be.

CXVI

O DAYS and hours, your work is this,
　　To hold me from my proper place,
　　A little while from his embrace,
For fuller gain of after bliss:

That out of distance might ensue
　　Desire of nearness doubly sweet;
　　And unto meeting, when we meet,
Delight a hundredfold accrue,

For every grain of sand that runs,
　　And every span of shade that steals,
　　And every kiss of toothed wheels,
And all the courses of the suns.

CXVII.

Contemplate all this work of Time,
    The giant labouring in his youth;
    Nor dream of human love and truth,
As dying Nature's earth and lime;

But trust that those we call the dead
    Are breathers of an ampler day
    For ever nobler ends.   They say,
The solid earth whereon we tread

In tracts of fluent heat began,
    And grew to seeming-random forms,
    The seeming prey of cyclic storms,
Till at the last arose the man;

Who throve and branch'd from clime to clime,
    The herald of a higher race,
    And of himself in higher place,
If so he type this work of time

Within himself, from more to more;
    Or, crown'd with attributes of woe
    Like glories, move his course, and show
That life is not as idle ore,

But iron dug from central gloom,
     And heated hot with burning fears,
     And dipt in baths of hissing tears,
And batter'd with the shocks of doom

To shape and use. Arise and fly
     The reeling Faun, the sensual feast;
     Move upward, working out the beast,
And let the ape and tiger die.

CXVIII.

Doors, where my heart was used to beat
      So quickly, not as one that weeps
      I come once more; the city sleeps;
I smell the meadow in the street;

I hear a chirp of birds; I see
      Betwixt the black fronts long-withdrawn
      A light blue lane of early dawn,
And think of early days and thee,

And bless thee, for thy lips are bland
      And bright the friendship of thine eye;
      And in my thoughts with scarce a sigh
I take the pressure of thine hand.

CXIX.

I TRUST I have not wasted breath:
  I think we are not wholly brain,
  Magnetic mockeries; not in vain,
Like Paul with beasts, I fought with Death;

Not only cunning casts in clay:
  Let Science prove we are, and then
  What matters Science unto men,
At least to me? I would not stay.

Let him, the wiser man who springs
  Hereafter, up from childhood shape
  His action like the greater ape,
But I was born to other things.

CXX.

Sad Hesper o'er the buried sun
    And ready, thou, to die with him,
    Thou watchest all things ever dim
And dimmer, and a glory done:

The team is loosen'd from the wain,
    The boat is drawn upon the shore;
    Thou listenest to the closing door,
And life is darken'd in the brain.

Bright Phosphor, fresher for the night,
    By thee the world's great work is heard
    Beginning, and the wakeful bird;
Behind thee comes the greater light:

The market boat is on the stream,
    And voices hail it from the brink;
    Thou hear'st the village hammer clink,
And see'st the moving of the team.

Sweet Hesper-Phosphor, double name
    For what is one, the first, the last,
    Thou, like my present and my past,
Thy place is changed; thou art the same.

CXXI.

Oh, wast thou with me, dearest, then,
　　While I rose up against my doom,
　　And yearn'd to burst the folded gloom,
To bare the eternal Heavens again,

To feel once more, in placid awe,
　　The strong imagination roll
　　A sphere of stars about my soul,
In all her motion one with law;

If thou wert with me, and the grave
　　Divide us not, be with me now,
　　And enter in at breast and brow,
Till all my blood, a fuller wave,

Be quicken'd with a livelier breath,
　　And like an inconsiderate boy,
　　As in the former flash of joy,
I slip the thoughts of life and death;

And all the breeze of Fancy blows,
　　And every dew-drop paints a bow,
　　The wizard lightnings deeply glow,
And every thought breaks out a rose.

CXXII.

There rolls the deep where grew the tree.
　　O earth, what changes hast thou seen!
　　There where the long street roars, hath been
The stillness of the central sea.

The hills are shadows, and they flow
　　From form to form, and nothing stands;
　　They melt like mist, the solid lands.
Like clouds they shape themselves and go.

But in my spirit will I dwell,
　　And dream my dream, and hold it true;
　　For tho' my lips may breathe adieu,
I cannot think the thing farewell.

CXXIII.

That which we dare invoke to bless;
    Our dearest faith; our ghastliest doubt;
    He, They, One, All; within, without;
The Power in darkness whom we guess;

I found Him not in world or sun,
    Or eagle's wing, or insect's eye;
    Nor thro' the questions men may try,
The petty cobwebs we have spun:

If e'er when faith had fall'n asleep,
    I heard a voice "believe no more"
    And heard an ever-breaking shore
That tumbled in the Godless deep;

A warmth within the breast would melt
    The freezing reason's colder part,
    And like a man in wrath the heart
Stood up and answer'd "I have felt."

No, like a child in doubt and fear:
    But that blind clamour made me wise;
    Then was I as a child that cries,
But, crying, knows his father near;

And what I am beheld again
    What is, and no man understands;
    And out of darkness came the hands
That reach thro' nature, moulding men.

CXXIV.

Whatever I have said or sung,
    Some bitter notes my harp would give,
    Yea, tho' there often seem'd to live
A contradiction on the tongue,

Yet Hope had never lost her youth;
    She did but look thro' dimmer eyes;
    Or Love but play'd with gracious lies,
Because he felt so fix'd in truth:

And if the song were full of care,
    He breathed the spirit of the song;
    And if the words were sweet and strong
He set his royal signet there;

Abiding with me till I sail
    To seek thee on the mystic deeps,
    And this electric force, that keeps
A thousand pulses dancing, fail.

CXIV.

Love is and was my Lord and King,
    And in his presence I attend
    To hear the tidings of my friend,
Which every hour his couriers bring.

Love is and was my King and Lord,
    And will be, tho' as yet I keep
    Within his court on earth, and sleep
Encompass'd by his faithful guard,

And hear at times a sentinel
    Who moves about from place to place,
    And whispers to the worlds of space,
In the deep night, that all is well.

CXXVI.

And all is well, tho' faith and form
    Be sunder'd in the night of fear;
    Well roars the storm to those that hear
A deeper voice across the storm,

Proclaiming social truth shall spread,
    And justice, ev'n tho' thrice again
    The red fool-fury of the Seine
Should pile her barricades with dead.

But ill for him that wears a crown,
    And him, the lazar, in his rags:
    They tremble, the sustaining crags;
The spires of ice are toppled down,

And molten up, and roar in flood;
    The fortress crashes from on high,
    The brute earth lightens to the sky,
And the great Æon sinks in blood,

And compass'd by the fires of Hell;
    While thou, dear spirit, happy star,
    O'erlook'st the tumult from afar,
And smilest, knowing all is well.

CXXVII.

The love that rose on stronger wings,
  Unpalsied when he met with Death,
  Is comrade of the lesser faith
That sees the course of human things.

No doubt vast eddies in the flood
  Of onward time shall yet be made,
  And throned races may degrade;
Yet O ye mysteries of good,

Wild Hours that fly with Hope and Fear,
  If all your office had to do
  With old results that look like new;
If this were all your mission here,

To draw, to sheathe a useless sword,
  To fool the crowd with glorious lies,
  To cleave a creed in sects and cries,
To change the bearing of a word,

To shift an arbitrary power,
  To cramp the student at his desk,
  To make old bareness picturesque
And tuft with grass a feudal tower;

Why then my scorn might well descend
  On you and yours. I see in part
  That all, as in some piece of art,
Is toil coöperant to an end.

CXXVIII.

Dear friend, far off, my lost desire,
    So far, so near in woe and weal;
    O loved the most, when most I feel
There is a lower and a higher;

Known and unknown; human, divine;
    Sweet human hand and lips and eye;
    Dear heavenly friend that canst not die,
Mine, mine, for ever, ever mine;

Strange friend, past, present, and to be;
    Loved deeplier, darklier understood;
    Behold, I dream a dream of good,
And mingle all the world with thee.

CXXIX.

Thy voice is on the rolling air;
　　I hear thee where the waters run;
　　Thou standest in the rising sun,
And in the setting thou art fair.

What art thou then?　I cannot guess;
　　But tho' I seem in star and flower
　　To feel thee some diffusive power,
I do not therefore love thee less:

My love involves the love before;
　　My love is vaster passion now;
　　Tho' mix'd with God and Nature thou,
I seem to love thee more and more.

Far off thou art, but ever nigh;
　　I have thee still, and I rejoice;
　　I prosper, circled with thy voice;
I shall not lose thee tho' I die.

CXXX.

O LIVING will that shalt endure
    When all that seems shall suffer shock,
    Rise in the spiritual rock,
Flow thro' our deeds and make them pure,

That we may lift from out of dust
    A voice as unto him that hears,
    A cry above the conquer'd years
To one that with us works, and trust,

With faith that comes of self-control,
    The truths that never can be proved
    Until we close with all we loved,
And all we flow from, soul in soul

O TRUE and tried, so well and long,
    Demand not thou a marriage lay;
    In that it is thy marriage day
Is music more than any song.

Nor have I felt so much of bliss
    Since first he told me that he loved
    A daughter of our house; nor proved
Since that dark day a day like this;

Tho' I since then have number'd o'er
    Some thrice three years: they went and came,
    Remade the blood and changed the frame,
And yet is love not less, but more;

No longer caring to embalm
    In dying songs a dead regret,
    But like a statue solid-set,
And moulded in colossal calm.

Regret is dead, but love is more
    Than in the summers that are flown,
    For I myself with these have grown
To something greater than before;

Which makes appear the songs I made
    As echoes out of weaker times,
    As half but idle brawling rhymes,
The sport of random sun and shade.

But where is she, the bridal flower,
    That must be made a wife ere noon?
    She enters, glowing like the moon
Of Eden on its bridal bower:

On me she bends her blissful eyes
    And then on thee; they meet thy look
    And brighten like the star that shook
Betwixt the palms of paradise.

O when her life was yet in bud,
    He too foretold the perfect rose.
    For thee she grew, for thee she grows
For ever, and as fair as good.

And thou art worthy; full of power;
    As gentle; liberal-minded, great,
    Consistent; wearing all that weight
Of learning lightly like a flower.

But now set out: the noon is near,
    And I must give away the bride;
    She fears not, or with thee beside
And me behind her, will not fear:

For I that danced her on my knee,
    That watch'd her on her nurse's arm,
    That shielded all her life from harm
At last must part with her to thee;

Now waiting to be made a wife,
    Her feet, my darling, on the dead;
    Their pensive tablets round' her head,
And the most living words of life

Breathed in her ear. The ring is on,
    The "wilt thou" answer'd, and again
    The "wilt thou" ask'd, till out of twain
Her sweet "I will" has made ye one.

Now sign your names, which shall be read,
    Mute symbols of a joyful morn,
    By village eyes as yet unborn;
The names are sign'd, and overhead

Begins the clash and clang that tells
    The joy to every wandering breeze;
    The blind wall rocks, and on the trees
The dead leaf trembles to the bells.

O happy hour, and happier hours
    Await them. Many a merry face
    Salutes them — maidens of the place,
That pelt us in the porch with flowers.

O happy hour, behold the bride
    With him to whom her hand I gave.
    They leave the porch, they pass the grave
That has to-day its sunny side.

To-day the grave is bright for me,
    For them the light of life increased,
    Who stay to share the morning feast,
Who rest to-night beside the sea.

Let all my genial spirits advance
    To meet and greet a whiter sun;
    My drooping memory will not shun
The foaming grape of eastern France.

It circles round, and fancy plays,
    And hearts are warm'd and faces bloom,
    As drinking health to bride and groom
We wish them store of happy days.

Nor count me all to blame if I
    Conjecture of a stiller guest,
    Perchance, perchance, among the rest,
And, tho' in silence, wishing joy.

But they must go, the time draws on,
    And those white-favour'd horses wait;
    They rise, but linger; it is late;
Farewell, we kiss, and they are gone.

A shade falls on us like the dark
    From little cloudlets on the grass,
    But sweeps away as out we pass
To range the woods, to roam the park,

Discussing how their courtship grew,
    And talk of others that are wed,
    And how she look'd, and what he said,
And back we come at fall of dew.

Again the feast, the speech, the glee,
    The shade of passing thought, the wealth
    Of words and wit, the double health,
The crowning cup, the three-times-three,

And last the dance; — till I retire:
    Dumb is that tower which spake so loud,
    And high in heaven the streaming cloud,
And on the downs a rising fire:

And rise, O moon, from yonder down,
    Till over down and over dale
    All night the shining vapour sail
And pass the silent-lighted town,

The white-faced halls, the glancing rills,
    And catch at every mountain head,
    And o'er the friths that branch and spread
Their sleeping silver thro' the hills;

And touch with shade the bridal doors,
With tender gloom the roof, the wall;
And breaking let the splendour fall
To spangle all the happy shores

By which they rest, and ocean sounds,
And, star and system rolling past,
A soul shall draw from out the vast
And strike his being into bounds,

And, moved thro' life of lower phase,
Result in man, be born and think,
And act and love, a closer link
Betwixt us and the crowning race

Of those that, eye to eye, shall look
On knowledge; under whose command
Is Earth and Earth's, and in their hand
Is Nature like an open book;

No longer half-akin to brute,
For all we thought and loved and did,
And hoped, and suffer'd, is but seed
Of what in them is flower and fruit;

Whereof the man, that with me trod
This planet, was a noble type
Appearing ere the times were ripe,
That friend of mine who lives in God,

That God, which ever lives and loves,
  One God, one law, one element,
  And one far-off divine event,
To which the whole creation moves.

THE PRINCESS.

A MEDLEY.

BY

ALFRED TENNYSON.

THE PRINCESS:
A MEDLEY.

PROLOGUE.

Sir Walter Vivian all a summer's day
Gave his broad lawns until the set of sun
Up to the people: thither flock'd at noon
His tenants, wife and child, and thither half
The neighbouring borough with their Institute
Of which he was the patron. I was there
From college, visiting the son, — the son
A Walter too, , — with others of our set,
Five others: we were seven at Vivian-place.

And me that morning Walter show'd the house,
Greek, set with busts: from vases in the hall
Flowers of all heavens, and lovelier than their names,
Grew side by side; and on the pavement lay
Carved stones of the Abbey-ruin in the park,
Huge Ammonites, and the first bones of Time;
And on the tables every clime and age
Jumbled together; celts and calumets,

Claymore and snowshoe, toys in lava, fans
Of sandal, amber, ancient rosaries,
Laborious orient ivory sphere in sphere,
The cursed Malayan crease, and battle-clubs
From the isles of palm: and higher on the walls,
Betwixt the monstrous horns of elk and deer,
His own forefathers' arms and armour hung.

    And "this" he said "was Hugh's at Agincourt;
And that was old Sir Ralph's at Ascalon:
A good knight he! we keep a chronicle
With all about him" — which he brought, and I
Dived in a hoard of tales that dealt with knights
Half-legend, half-historic, counts and kings
Who laid about them at their wills and died;
And mixt with these, a lady, one that arm'd
Her own fair head, and sallying thro' the gate,
Had beat her foes with slaughter from her walls.

    "O miracle of women," said the book,
"O noble heart who, being strait-besieged
By this wild king to force her to his wish,
Nor bent, nor broke, nor shunn'd a soldier's death,
But now when all was lost or seem'd as lost —
Her stature more than mortal in the burst
Of sunrise, her arm lifted, eyes on fire —
Broke with a blast of trumpets from the gate,
And, falling on them like a thunderbolt,

She trampled some beneath her horses' heels,
And some were whelm'd with missiles of the wall,
And some were push'd with lances from the rock,
And part were drown'd within the whirling brook:
O miracle of noble womanhood!"

So sang the gallant glorious chronicle;
And, I all rapt in this, "Come out," he said,
"To the Abbey: there is Aunt Elizabeth
And sister Lilia with the rest."   We went
(I kept the book and had my finger in it)
Down thro' the park: strange was the sight to me;
For all the sloping pasture murmur'd, sown
With happy faces and with holiday.
There moved the multitude, a thousand heads:
The patient leaders of their Institute
Taught them with facts.   One rear'd a font of stone
And drew, from butts of water on the slope,
The fountain of the moment, playing now
A twisted snake, and now a rain of pearls,
Or steep-up spout whereon the gilded ball
Danced like a wisp: and somewhat lower down
A man with knobs and wires and vials fired
A cannon: Echo answer'd in her sleep
From hollow fields: and here were telescopes
For azure views; and there a group of girls
In circle waited, whom the electric shock
Dislink'd with shrieks and laughter: round the lake

A little clock-work steamer paddling plied
And shook the lilies: perch'd about the knolls
A dozen angry models jetted steam:
A petty railway ran: a fire-balloon
Rose gem-like up before the dusky groves
And dropt a fairy parachute and past:
And there thro' twenty posts of telegraph
They flash'd a saucy message to and fro
Between the mimic stations; so that sport
Went hand in hand with Science; otherwhere
Pure sport: a herd of boys with clamour bowl'd
And stump'd the wicket; babies roll'd about
Like tumbled fruit in grass; and men and maids
Arranged a country dance, and flew thro' light
And shadow, while the twangling violin
Struck up with Soldier-laddie, and overhead
The broad ambrosial aisles of lofty lime
Made noise with bees and breeze from end to end.

Strange was the sight and smacking of the time;
And long we gazed, but satiated at length
Came to the ruins. High-arch'd and ivy-claspt,
Of finest Gothic lighter than a fire,
Thro' one wide chasm of time and frost they gave
The park, the crowd, the house; but all within
The sward was trim as any garden lawn:
And here we lit on Aunt Elizabeth,
And Lilia with the rest, and lady friends

From neighbour seats: and there was Ralph himself,
A broken statue propt against the wall,
As gay as any.   Lilia, wild with sport,
Half child half woman as she was, had wound
A scarf of orange round the stony helm,
And robed the shoulders in a rosy silk,
That made the old warrior from his ivied nook
Glow like a sunbeam: near his tomb a feast
Shone, silver-set; about it lay the guests,
And there we join'd them: then the maiden Aunt
Took this fair day for text, and from it preach'd
An universal culture for the crowd,
And all things great; but we, unworthier, told
Of college: he had climb'd across the spikes,
And he had squeezed himself betwixt the bars,
And he had breathed the Proctor's dogs; and one
Discuss'd his tutor, rough to common men,
But honeying at the whisper of a lord;
And one the Master, as a rogue in grain
Veneer'd with sanctimonious theory.

But while they talk'd, above their heads I saw
The feudal warrior lady-clad; which brought
My book to mind: and opening this I read
Of old Sir Ralph a page or two that rang
With tilt and tourney; then the tale of her
That drove her foes with slaughter from her walls,
And much I praised her nobleness, and "Where,"

Ask'd Walter, patting Lilia's head (she lay
Beside him) "lives there such a woman now?"

Quick answer'd Lilia "There are thousands now
Such women, but convention beats them down:
It is but bringing up; no more than that:
You men have done it: how I hate you all!
Ah, were I something great! I wish I were
Some mighty poetess, I would shame you then,
That love to keep us children! O I wish
That I were some great Princess, I would build
Far off from men a college like a man's,
And I would teach them all that men are taught;
We are twice as quick!" And here she shook aside
The hand that play'd the patron with her curls.

And one said smiling "Pretty were the sight
If our old halls could change their sex, and flaunt
With prudes for proctors, dowagers for deans,
And sweet girl-graduates in their golden hair.
I think they should not wear our rusty gowns,
But move as rich as Emperor-moths, or Ralph
Who shines so in the corner; yet I fear,
If there were many Lilias in the brood,
However deep you might embower the nest,
Some boy would spy it."
                              At this upon the sward
She tapt her tiny silken-sandal'd foot:

"That's your light way; but I would make it death
For any male thing but to peep at us."

  Petulant she spoke, and at herself she laugh'd;
A rosebud set with little wilful thorns,
And sweet as English air could make her, she:
But Walter hail'd a score of names upon her,
And "petty Ogress," and "ungrateful Puss,"
And swore he long'd at college, only long'd,
All else was well, for she-society.
They boated and they cricketed; they talk'd
At wine, in clubs, of art, of politics;
They lost their weeks; they vext the souls of deans;
They rode; they betted; made a hundred friends,
And caught the blossom of the flying terms,
But miss'd the mignonette of Vivian-place,
The little hearth-flower Lilia.   Thus he spoke,
Part banter, part affection.

      "True," she said,
"We doubt not that.   O yes, you miss'd us much.
I'll stake my ruby ring upon it you did."

  She held it out; and as a parrot turns
Up thro' gilt wires a crafty loving eye,
And takes a lady's finger with all care,
And bites it for true heart and not for harm,
So he with Lilia's.   Daintily she shriek'd
And wrung it.   "Doubt my word again!" he said.

"Come, listen! here is proof that you were miss'd:
We seven stay'd at Christmas up to read;
And there we took one tutor as to read:
The hard-grain'd Muses of the cube and square
Were out of season: never man, I think,
So moulder'd in a sinecure as he:
For while our cloisters echo'd frosty feet,
And our long walks were stript as bare as brooms,
We did but talk you over, pledge you all
In wassail; often, like as many girls —
Sick for the hollies and the yews of home —
As many little trifling Lilias — play'd
Charades and riddles as at Christmas here,
And *what's my thought* and *when* and *where* and *how*,
And often told a tale from mouth to mouth
As here at Christmas."

                She remember'd that :
A pleasant game, she thought: she liked it more
Than magic music, forfeits, all the rest.
But these — what kind of tales did men tell men,
She wonder'd, by themselves?

                  A half-disdain
Perch'd on the pouted blossom of her lips:
And Walter nodded at me; "*He* began,
The rest would follow, each in turn; and so
We forged a sevenfold story.　Kind? what kind?
Chimeras, crotchets, Christmas solecisms,
Seven-headed monsters only made to kill

Time by the fire in winter."

               "Kill him now,
The tyrant! kill him in the summer too,"
Said Lilia; "Why not now," the maiden Aunt.
"Why not a summer's as a winter's tale?
A tale for summer as befits the time,
And something it should be to suit the place,
Heroic, for a hero lies beneath,
Grave, solemn!"

               Walter warp'd his mouth at this
To something so mock-solemn, that I laugh'd
And Lilia woke with sudden-shrilling mirth
An echo like a ghostly woodpecker,
Hid in the ruins; till the maiden Aunt
(A little sense of wrong had touch'd her face
With colour) turn'd to me with "As you will;
Heroic if you will, or what you will,
Or be yourself your hero if you will."

    "Take Lilia, then, for heroine" clamour'd he,
"And make her some great Princess, six feet high,
Grand, epic, homicidal; and be you
The Prince to win her!"

               "Then follow me, the Prince,"
I answer'd, "each be hero in his turn!
Seven and yet one, like shadows in a dream. —
Heroic seems our Princess as required. —
But something made to suit with Time and place,

A Gothic ruin and a Grecian house,
A talk of college and of ladies' rights,
A feudal knight in silken masquerade,
And, yonder, shrieks and strange experiments
For which the good Sir Ralph had burnt them all —
This *were* a medley! we should have him back
Who told the "Winter's tale" to do it for us.
No matter: we will say whatever comes.
And let the ladies sing us, if they will,
From time to time, some ballad or a song
To give us breathing-space."

                    So I began,
And the rest follow'd: and the women sang
Between the rougher voices of the men,
Like linnets in the pauses of the wind:
And here I give the story and the songs.

I.

A Prince I was, blue-eyed, and fair in face,
Of temper amorous, as the first of May,
With lengths of yellow ringlet, like a girl,
For on my cradle shone the Northern star.

There lived an ancient legend in our house.
Some sorcerer, whom a far-off grandsire burnt
Because he cast no shadow, had foretold,
Dying, that none of all our blood should know
The shadow from the substance, and that one
Should come to fight with shadows and to fall.
For so, my mother said, the story ran.
And, truly, waking dreams were, more or less,
An old and strange affection of the house.
Myself too had weird seizures, Heaven knows what:
On a sudden in the midst of men and day,
And while I walk'd and talk'd as heretofore,
I seem'd to move among a world of ghosts,
And feel myself the shadow of a dream.
Our great court-Galen poised his gilt-head cane,
And paw'd his beard, and mutter'd "catalepsy."
My mother pitying made a thousand prayers;
My mother was as mild as any saint,

Half-canonized by all that look'd on her,
So gracious was her tact and tenderness:
But my good father thought a king a king;
He cared not for the affection of the house;
He held his sceptre like a pedant's wand
To lash offence, and with long arms and hands
Reach'd out, and pick'd offenders from the mass
For judgment.
   Now it chanced that I had been,
While life was yet in bud and blade, betroth'd
To one, a neighbouring Princess: she to me
Was proxy-wedded with a bootless calf
At eight years old; and still from time to time
Came murmurs of her beauty from the South,
And of her brethren, youths of puissance;
And still I wore her picture by my heart,
And one dark tress; and all around them both
Sweet thoughts would swarm as bees about their queen.

But when the days drew nigh that I should wed,
My father sent ambassadors with furs
And jewels, gifts, to fetch her: these brought back
A present, a great labour of the loom;
And therewithal an answer vague as wind:
Besides, they saw the king; he took the gifts;
He said there was a compact; that was true:
But then she had a will; was he to blame?

And maiden fancies; loved to live alone
Among her women; certain, would not wed.

That morning in the presence room I stood
With Cyril and with Florian, my two friends:
The first, a gentleman of broken means
(His father's fault) but given to starts and bursts
Of revel; and the last, my other heart,
And almost my half-self, for still we moved
Together, twinn'd as horse's ear and eye.

Now, while they spake, I saw my father's face
Grow long and troubled like a rising moon,
Inflamed with wrath: he started on his feet,
Tore the king's letter, snow'd it down, and rent
The wonder of the loom thro' warp and woof
From skirt to skirt; and at the last he sware
That he would send a hundred thousand men,
And bring her in a whirlwind: then he chew'd
The thrice-turn'd cud of wrath, and cook'd his spleen,
Communing with his captains of the war.

At last I spoke. "My father, let me go.
It cannot be but some gross error lies
In this report, this answer of a king,
Whom all men rate as kind and hospitable:
Or, maybe, I myself, my bride once seen,
Whate'er my grief to find her less than fame,

May rue the bargain made."   And Florian said:
"I have a sister at the foreign court,
Who moves about the Princess; she, you know,
Who wedded with a nobleman from thence:
He, dying lately, left her, as I hear,
The lady of three castles in that land:
Thro' her this matter might be sifted clean."
And Cyril whisper'd: "Take me with you too."
Then laughing "what, if these weird seizures come
Upon you in those lands, and no one near
To point you out the shadow from the truth!
Take me: I'll serve you better in a strait;
I grate on rusty hinges here:" but "No!"
Roar'd the rough king, "you shall not; we ourself
Will crush her pretty maiden fancies dead
In iron gauntlets: break the council up."

　　But when the council broke, I rose and past
Thro' the wild woods that hung about the town;
Found a still place, and pluck'd her likeness out;
Laid it on flowers, and watch'd it lying bathed
In the green gleam of dewy-tassell'd trees:
What were those fancies? wherefore break her troth?
Proud look'd the lips: but while I meditated
A wind arose and rush'd upon the South,
And shook the songs, the whispers, and the shrieks
Of the wild woods together; and a Voice
Went with it "Follow, follow, thou shalt win."

Then, ere the silver sickle of that month
Became her golden shield, I stole from court
With Cyril and with Florian, unperceived,
Cat-footed thro' the town and half in dread
To hear my father's clamour at our backs
With Ho! from some bay-window shake the night;
But all was quiet: from the bastion'd walls
Like threaded spiders, one by one, we dropt,
And flying reach'd the frontier: then we crost
To a livelier land; and so by tilth and grange,
And vines, and blowing bosks of wilderness,
We gain'd the mother-city thick with towers,
And in the imperial palace found the king.

His name was Gama; crack'd and small his voice,
But bland the smile that like a wrinkling wind
On glassy water drove his cheek in lines;
A little dry old man, without a star,
Not like a king: three days he feasted us,
And on the fourth I spake of why we came,
And my betroth'd. "You do us, Prince," he said,
Airing a snowy hand and signet gem,
"All honour. We remember love ourselves
In our sweet youth: there did a compact pass
Long summers back, a kind of ceremony —
I think the year in which our olives fail'd.
I would you had her, Prince, with all my heart,
With my full heart: but there were widows here,

Two widows, Lady Psyche, Lady Blanche;
They fed her theories, in and out of place
Maintaining that with equal husbandry
The woman were an equal to the man.
They harp'd on this; with this our banquets rang;
Our dances broke and buzz'd in knots of talk;
Nothing but this; my very ears were hot
To hear them: knowledge, so my daughter held,
Was all in all; they had but been, she thought,
As children; they must lose the child, assume
The woman: then, Sir, awful odes she wrote,
Too awful, sure, for what they treated of,
But all she is and does is awful; odes
About this losing of the child; and rhymes
And dismal lyrics, prophesying change
Beyond all reason: these the women sang;
And they that know such things — I sought but peace;
No critic I — would call them masterpieces:
They master'd me.   At last she begg'd a boon
A certain summer-palace which I have
Hard by your father's frontier: I said no,
Yet being an easy man, gave it; and there,
All wild to found an University
For maidens, on the spur she fled; and more
We know not, — only this: they see no men,
Not ev'n her brother Arac, nor the twins
Her brethren, tho' they love her, look upon her
As on a kind of paragon; and I

(Pardon me saying it) were much loth to breed
Dispute betwixt myself and mine: but since
(And I confess with right) you think me bound
In some sort, I can give you letters to her;
And yet, to speak the truth, I rate your chance
Almost at naked nothing."
                              Thus the king;
And I, tho' nettled that he seem'd to slur
With garrulous ease and oily courtesies
Our formal compact, yet, not less (all frets
But chafing me on fire to find my bride)
Went forth again with both my friends. We rode
Many a long league back to the North. At last
From hills, that look'd across a land of hope,
We dropt with evening on a rustic town
Set in a gleaming river's crescent-curve,
Close at the boundary of the liberties;
There, enter'd an old hostel, call'd mine host
To council, plied him with his richest wines,
And show'd the late-writ letters of the king.

    He with a long low sibilation, stared
As blank as death in marble; then exclaim'd
Averring it was clear against all rules
For any man to go: but as his brain
Began to mellow, "If the king," he said,
"Had given us letters, was he bound to speak?
The king would bear him out;" and at the last —

The summer of the vine in all his veins —
"No doubt that we might make it worth his while.
She once had past that way; he heard her speak;
She scared him; life! he never saw the like;
She look'd as grand as doomsday and as grave:
And he, he reverenced his liege-lady there;
He always made a point to post with mares;
His daughter and his housemaid were the boys:
The land, he understood, for miles about
Was till'd by women; all the swine were sows,
And all the dogs" —
                              But while he jested thus,
A thought flash'd thro' me which I clothed in act,
Remembering how we three presented Maid
Or Nymph, or Goddess, at high tide of feast,
In masque or pageant at my father's court.
We sent mine host to purchase female gear;
He brought it, and himself, a sight to shake
The midriff of despair with laughter, holp
To lace us up, till, each, in maiden plumes
We rustled: him we gave a costly bribe
To guerdon silence, mounted our good steeds,
And boldly ventured on the liberties.

We follow'd up the river as we rode,
And rode till midnight when the college lights
Began to glitter firefly-like in copse
And linden alley: then we past an arch,

Whereon a woman-statue rose with wings
From four wing'd horses dark against the stars;
And some inscription ran along the front,
But deep in shadow: further on we gain'd
A little street half garden and half house;
But scarce could hear each other speak for noise
Of clocks and chimes, like silver hammers falling
On silver anvils, and the splash and stir
Of fountains spouted up and showering down
In meshes of the jasmine and the rose:
And all about us peal'd the nightingale,
Rapt in her song, and careless of the snare.

There stood a bust of Pallas for a sign,
By two sphere lamps blazon'd like Heaven and Earth
With constellation and with continent,
Above an entry: riding in, we call'd;
A plump-arm'd Ostleress and a stable wench
Came running at the call, and help'd us down.
Then stept a buxom hostess forth, and sail'd,
Full-blown, before us into rooms which gave
Upon a pillar'd porch, the bases lost
In laurel: her we ask'd of that and this,
And who were tutors. "Lady Blanche" she said,
"And Lady Psyche." "Which was prettiest,
Best-natured?" "Lady Psyche." "Here are we,"
One voice, we cried; and I sat down and wrote,

In such a hand as when a field of corn
Bows all its ears before the roaring East;

    "'Three ladies of the Northern empire pray
Your Highness would enroll them with your own,
As Lady Psyche's pupils."
                            This I seal'd:
The seal was Cupid bent above a scroll,
And o'er his head Uranian Venus hung,
And raised the blinding bandage from his eyes:
I gave the letter to be sent with dawn;
And then to bed, where half in doze I seem'd
To float about a glimmering night, and watch
A full sea glazed with muffled moonlight, swell
On some dark shore just seen that it was rich.

As thro' the land at eve we went,
  And pluck'd the ripen'd ears,
We fell out, my wife and I,
O we fell out I know not why,
  And kiss'd again with tears.

For when we came where lies the child
  We lost in other years,
There above the little grave,
O there above the little grave,
  We kiss'd again with tears.

II.

At break of day the College Portress came:
She brought us Academic silks, in hue
The lilac, with a silken hood to each,
And zoned with gold; and now when these were on,
And we as rich as moths from dusk cocoons,
She, curtseying her obeisance, let us know
The Princess Ida waited: out we paced,
I first, and following thro' the porch that sang
All round with laurel, issued in a court
Compact of lucid marbles, boss'd with lengths
Of classic frieze, with ample awnings gay
Betwixt the pillars, and with great urns of flowers.
The Muses and the Graces, group'd in threes,
Enring'd a billowing fountain in the midst;
And here and there on lattice edges lay
Or book or lute; but hastily we past,
And up a flight of stairs into the hall.

There at a board by tome and paper sat,
With two tame leopards couch'd beside her throne,
All beauty compass'd in a female form,
The Princess; liker to the inhabitant
Of some clear planet close upon the Sun,

Than our man's earth; such eyes were in her head,
And so much grace and power, breathing down
From over her arch'd brows, with every turn
Lived thro' her to the tips of her long hands,
And to her feet. She rose her height, and said:

"We give you welcome: not without redound
Of use and glory to yourselves ye come,
The first-fruits of the stranger: aftertime,
And that full voice which circles round the grave,
Will rank you nobly, mingled up with me.
What! are the ladies of your land so tall?"
"We of the court" said Cyril. "From the court"
She answer'd, "then ye know the Prince?" and he:
"The climax of his age! as tho' there were
One rose in all the world, your Highness that,
He worships your ideal:" she replied:
"We scarcely thought in our own hall to hear
This barren verbiage, current among men,
Light coin, the tinsel clink of compliment. ·
Your flight from out your bookless wilds would seem
As arguing love of knowledge and of power;
Your language proves you still the child. Indeed,
We dream not of him: when we set our hand
To this great work, we purposed with ourselves
Never to wed. You likewise will do well,
Ladies, in entering here, to cast and fling
The tricks, which make us toys of men, that so,

Some future time, if so indeed you will,
You may with those self-styled our lords ally
Your fortunes, justlier balanced, scale with scale."

At those high words, we conscious of ourselves,
Perused the matting; then an officer
Rose up, and read the statutes, such as these:
Not for three years to correspond with home;
Not for three years to cross the liberties;
Not for three years to speak with any men;
And many more, which hastily subscribed,
We enter'd on the boards: and "Now" she cried
"Ye are green wood, see ye warp not. Look, our hall!
Our statues! — not of those that men desire,
Sleek Odalisques, or oracles of mode,
Nor stunted squaws of West or East; but she
That taught the Sabine how to rule, and she
The foundress of the Babylonian wall,
The Carian Artemisia strong in war,
The Rhodope, that built the pyramid
Clelia, Cornelia, with the Palmyrene
That fought Aurelian, and the Roman brows
Of Agrippina. Dwell with these, and lose
Convention, since to look on noble forms
Makes noble thro' the sensuous organism
That which is higher. O lift your natures up:
Embrace our aims: work out your freedom. Girls,
Knowledge is now no more a fountain seal'd:

Drink deep, until the habits of the slave,
The sins of emptiness, gossip and spite
And slander, die.   Better not be at all
Than not be noble.   Leave us: you may go:
To-day the Lady Psyche will harangue
The fresh arrivals of the week before;
For they press in from all the provinces,
And fill the hive."
                       She spoke, and bowing waved
Dismissal: back again we crost the court
To Lady Psyche's: as we enter'd in,
There sat along the forms, like morning doves
That sun their milky bosoms on the thatch,
A patient range of pupils; she herself
Erect behind a desk of satin-wood,
A quick brunette, well-moulded, falcon-eyed,
And on the hither side, or so she look'd,
Of twenty summers.   At her left, a child,
In shining draperies, headed like a star,
Her maiden babe, a double April old,
Aglaïa slept.   We sat: the Lady glanced:
Then Florian, but no livelier than the dame,
That whisper'd "Asses ears" among the sedge,
"My sister."   "Comely too by all that's fair"
Said Cyril.   "O hush, hush!" and she began.

"This world was once a fluid haze of light,
Till toward the centre set the starry tides,
                13*

And eddied into suns, that wheeling cast
The planets: then the monster, then the man;
T'attoo'd or woaded, winter-clad in skins,
Raw from the prime, and crushing down his mate;
As yet we find in barbarous isles, and here
Among the lowest."
              Thereupon she took
A bird's-eye-view of all the ungracious past;
Glanced at the legendary Amazon
As emblematic of a nobler age;
Appraised the Lycian custom, spoke of those
That lay at wine with Lar and Lucumo;
Ran down the Persian, Grecian, Roman lines
Of empire, and the woman's state in each,
How far from just; till warming with her theme
She fulmined out her scorn of laws Salique
And little-footed China, touch'd on Mahomet
With much contempt, and came to chivalry:
When some respect, however slight, was paid
To woman, superstition all awry:
However then commenced the dawn: a beam
Had slanted forward, falling in a land
Of promise; fruit would follow. Deep, indeed,
Their debt of thanks to her who first had dared
To leap the rotten pales of prejudice,
Disyoke their necks from custom, and assert
None lordlier than themselves but that which made
Woman and man. She had founded; they must build.

Here might they learn whatever men were taught:
Let them not fear: some said their heads were less:
Some men's were small; not they the least of men;
For often fineness compensated size:
Besides the brain was like the hand, and grew
With using; thence the man's, if more, was more;
He took advantage of his strength to be
First in the field: some ages had been lost;
But woman ripen'd earlier, and her life
Was longer; and albeit their glorious names
Were fewer, scatter'd stars, yet since in truth
The highest is the measure of the man,
And not the Kaffir, Hottentot, Malay,
Nor those horn-handed breakers of the globe,
But Homer, Plato, Verulam; even so
With woman: and in arts of government
Elizabeth and others; arts of war
The peasant Joan and others; arts of grace
Sappho and others vied with any man:
And, last not least, she who had left her place,
And bow'd her state to them, that they might grow
To use and power on this Oasis, lapt
In the arms of leisure, sacred from the blight
Of ancient influence and scorn.

       At last.
She rose upon a wind of prophecy
Dilating on the future: "everywhere
Two heads in council, two beside the hearth,

Two in the tangled business of the world,
Two in the liberal offices of life,
Two plummets dropt for one to sound the abyss
Of science, and the secrets of the mind:
Musician, painter, sculptor, critic, more:
And everywhere the broad and bounteous Earth
Should bear a double growth of those rare souls,
Poets, whose thoughts enrich the blood of the world."

       She ended here, and beckon'd us: the rest
Parted; and, glowing full-faced welcome, she
Began to address us, and was moving on
In gratulation, till as when a boat
Tacks, and the slacken'd sail flaps, all her voice
Faltering and fluttering in her throat, she cried
"My brother!" "Well, my sister." "O" she said
"What do you here? and in this dress? and these?
Why who are these? a wolf within the fold!
A pack of wolves! the Lord be gracious to me!
A plot, a plot, a plot to ruin all!"
"No plot, no plot," he answer'd. "Wretched boy,
How saw you not the inscription on the gate,
LET NO MAN ENTER IN ON PAIN OF DEATH?"
"And if I had" he answer'd "who could think
The softer Adams of your Academe,
O sister, Sirens tho' they be, were such
As chanted on the blanching bones of men?"
"But you will find it otherwise" she said.

"You jest: ill jesting with edge-tools! my vow
Binds me to speak, and O that iron will,
That axelike edge unturnable, our Head,
The Princess." "Well then, Psyche, take my life,
And nail me like a weasel on a grange
For warning: bury me beside the gate,
And cut this epitaph above my bones;
Here lies a brother by a sister slain,
All for the common good of womankind."
"Let me die too" said Cyril "having seen
And heard the Lady Psyche."

                   I struck in:
"Albeit so mask'd, Madam, I love the truth;
Receive it; and in me behold the Prince
Your countryman, affianced years ago
To the Lady Ida: here, for here she was,
And thus (what other way was left) I came."
"O Sir, O Prince, I have no country; none;
If any, this; but none. Whate'er I was
Disrooted, what I am is grafted here.
Affianced, Sir? love-whispers may not breathe
Within this vestal limit, and how should I,
Who am not mine, say, live: the thunderbolt
Hangs silent; but prepare: I speak; it falls."
"Yet pause," I said: "for that inscription there,
I think no more of deadly lurks therein,
Than in a clapper clapping in a garth,
To scare the fowl from fruit: if more there be,

If more and acted on, what follows? war;
Your own work marr'd: for this your Academe,
Whichever side be Victor, in the balloo
Will topple to the trumpet down, and pass
With all fair theories only made to gild
A stormless summer."   "Let the Princess judge
Of that" she said: "farewell Sir — and to you.
I shudder at the sequel, but I go."

"Are you that Lady Psyche" I rejoin'd,
"The fifth in line from that old Florian,
Yet hangs his portrait in my father's hall
(The gaunt old Baron with his beetle brow
Sun-shaded in the heat of dusty fights)
As he bestrode my Grandsire, when he fell,
And all else fled: we point to it, and we say,
The loyal warmth of Florian is not cold,
But branches current yet in kindred veins."
"Are you that Psyche" Florian added "she
With whom I sang about the morning hills,
Flung ball, flew kite, and raced the purple fly,
And snared the squirrel of the glen? are you
That Psyche, wont to bind my throbbing brow,
To smoothe my pillow, mix the foaming draught
Of fever, tell me pleasant tales, and read
My sickness down to happy dreams? are you
That brother-sister Psyche, both in one?
You were that Psyche, but what are you now?"

"You are that Psyche," Cyril said, "for whom
I would be that for ever which I seem
Woman, if I might sit beside your feet,
And glean your scatter'd sapience."

                             Then once more,
"Are you that Lady Psyche" I began,
"That on her bridal morn before she past
From all her old companions, when the king
Kiss'd her pale cheek, declared that ancient ties
Would still be dear beyond the southern hills;
That were there any of our people there
In want or peril, there was one to hear
And help them: look! for such are these and I."
"Are you that Psyche" Florian ask'd "to whom,
In gentler days, your arrow-wounded fawn
Came flying while you sat beside the well?
The creature laid his muzzle on your lap,
And sobb'd, and you sobb'd with it, and the blood
Was sprinkled on your kirtle, and you wept.
That was fawn's blood, not brother's, yet you wept.
O by the bright head of my little niece,
You were that Psyche, and what are you now?"
"You are that Psyche" Cyril said again,
"The mother of the sweetest little maid,
That ever crow'd for kisses."

                             "Out upon it!"
She answer'd, "peace! and why should I not play
The Spartan Mother with emotion, be

The Lucius Junius Brutus of my kind?
Him you call great: he for the common weal,
The fading politics of mortal Rome,
As I might slay this child, if good need were,
Slew both his sons: and I, shall I, on whom
The secular emancipation turns
Of half this world, be swerved from right to save
A prince, a brother? a little will I yield.
Best so, perchance, for us, and well for you.
O hard, when love and duty clash! I fear
My conscience will not count me fleckless; yet —
Hear my conditions: promise (otherwise
You perish) as you came to slip away,
To-day, to-morrow, soon: it shall be said,
These women were too barbarous, would not learn;
They fled, who might have shamed us: promise, all."

    What could we else, we promised each; and she,
Like some wild creature newly-caged, commenced
A to-and-fro, so pacing till she paused
By Florian; holding out her lily arms
Took both his hands, and smiling faintly said:
"I knew you at the first: tho' you have grown
You scarce have alter'd: I am sad and glad
To see you, Florian. I give thee to death
My brother! it was duty spoke, not I.
My needful seeming harshness, pardon it.

Our mother, is she well?"
                         With that she kiss'd
His forehead, then, a moment after, clung
About him, and betwixt them blossom'd up
From out a common vein of memory
Sweet household talk, and phrases of the hearth,
And far allusion, till the gracious dews
Began to glisten and to fall: and while
They stood, so rapt, we gazing, came a voice,
"I brought a message here from Lady Blanche."
Back started she, and turning round we saw
The Lady Blanche's daughter where she stood,
Melissa, with her hand upon the lock,
A rosy blonde, and in a college gown,
That clad her like an April daffodilly
(Her mother's colour) with her lips apart,
And all her thoughts as fair within her eyes,
As bottom agates seen to wave and float
In crystal currents of clear morning seas.

     So stood that same fair creature at the door.
Then Lady Psyche "Ah — Melissa — you!
You heard us?" and Melissa, "O pardon me!
I heard, I could not help it, did not wish:
But, dearest Lady, pray you fear me not,
Nor think I bear that heart within my breast,

To give three gallant gentlemen to death."
"I trust you" said the other "for we two
Were always friends, none closer, elm and vine:
But yet your mother's jealous temperament —
Let not your prudence, dearest, drowse, or prove
The Danaïd of a leaky vase, for fear
This whole foundation ruin, and I lose
My honour, these their lives.". "Ah, fear me not"
Replied Melissa "no — I would not tell,
No, not for all Aspasia's cleverness,
No, not to answer, Madam, all those hard things
That Sheba came to ask of Solomon."
"Be it so" the other "that we still may lead
The new light up, and culminate in peace,
For Solomon may come to Sheba yet."
Said Cyril "Madam, he the wisest man
Feasted the woman wisest then, in halls
Of Lebanonian cedar: nor should you
(Tho' madam *you* should answer, *we* would ask)
Less welcome find among us, if you came
Among us, debtors for our lives to you,
Myself for something more." He said not what,
But "Thanks," she answer'd "go: we have been too long
Together: keep your hoods about the face;
They do so that affect abstraction here.
Speak little; mix not with the rest; and hold
Your promise: all, I trust, may yet be well."

We turn'd to go, but Cyril took the child,
And held her round the knees against his waist,
And blew the swoll'n cheek of a trumpeter,
While Psyche watch'd them, smiling, and the child
Push'd her flat hand against his face and laugh'd;
And thus our conference closed.

                        And then we stroll'd
For half the day thro' stately theatres
Bench'd crescent-wise.   In each we sat, we heard
The grave Professor.   On the lecture slate
The circle rounded under female hands
With flawless demonstration: follow'd then
A classic lecture, rich in sentiment,
With scraps of thundrous Epic lilted out
By violet-hooded Doctors, elegies
And quoted odes, and jewels five-words-long
That on the stretch'd forefinger of all Time
Sparkle for ever: then we dipt in all
That treats of whatsoever is, the state,
The total chronicles of man, the mind,
The morals, something of the frame, the rock,
The star, the bird, the fish, the shell, the flower,
Electric, chemic laws, and all the rest,
And whatsoever can be taught and known;
Till like three horses that have broken fence,
And glutted all night long breast-deep in corn,
We issued gorged with knowledge, and I spoke:

"Why, Sirs, they do all this as well as we."
"They hunt old trails" said Cyril "very well
But when did woman ever yet invent?"
"Ungracious!" answer'd Florian, "have you learnt
No more from Psyche's lecture, you that talk'd
The trash that made me sick, and almost sad?"
"O trash" he said "but with a kernel in it.
Should I not call her wise, who made me wise?
And learnt? I learnt more from her in a flash,
Than if my brainpan were an empty hull,
And every Muse tumbled a science in.
A thousand hearts lie fallow in these halls,
And round these halls a thousand baby loves
Fly twanging headless arrows at the hearts,
Whence follows many a vacant pang; but O
With me, Sir, enter'd in the bigger boy,
The Head of all the golden-shafted firm,
The long-limb'd lad that had a Psyche too;
He cleft me thro' the stomacher; and now
What think you of it, Florian? do I chase
The substance or the shadow? will it hold?
I have no scorcerer's malison on me,
No ghostly hauntings like his Highness. I
Flatter myself that always everywhere
I know the substance when I see it. Well,
Are castles shadows? Three of them? Is she
The sweet proprietress a shadow? If not,

Shall those three castles patch my tatter'd coat?
For dear are those three castles to my wants,
And dear is sister Psyche to my heart,
And two dear things are one of double worth,
And much I might have said, but that my zone
Unmann'd me: then the Doctors! O to hear
The Doctors! O to watch the thirsty plants
Imbibing! once or twice I thought to roar,
To break my chain, to shake my mane: but thou,
Modulate me, Soul of mincing mimicry!
Make liquid treble of that bassoon, my throat;
Abase those eyes that ever loved to meet
Star-sisters answering under crescent brows;
Abate the stride, which speaks of man, and loose
A flying charm of blushes o'er this cheek,
Where they like swallows coming out of time
Will wonder why they came: but hark the bell
For dinner, let us go!"
     And in we stream'd
Among the columns, pacing staid and still
By twos and threes, till all from end to end
With beauties every shade of brown and fair,
In colours gayer than the morning mist,
The long hall glitter'd like a bed of flowers.
How might a man not wander from his wits
Pierced thro' with eyes, but that I kept mine own
Intent on her, who rapt in glorious dreams,

The second-sight of some Astræan age,
Sat compass'd with professors: they, the while,
Discuss'd a doubt and tost it to and fro:
A clamour thicken'd, mixt with inmost terms
Of art and science: Lady Blanche alone
Of faded form and haughtiest lineaments,
With all her Autumn tresses falsely brown,
Shot sidelong daggers at us, a tiger-cat
In act to spring.

                At last a solemn grace
Concluded, and we sought the gardens: there
One walk'd reciting by herself, and one
In this hand held a volume as to read,
And smoothed a petted peacock down with that:
Some to a low song oar'd a shallop by,
Or under arches of the marble bridge
Hung, shadow'd from the heat: some hid and sought
In the orange thickets: others tost a ball
Above the fountain-jets, and back again
With laughter: others lay about the lawns,
Of the older sort, and murmur'd that their May
Was passing: what was learning unto them?
They wish'd to marry; they could rule a house;
Men hated learned women; but we three
Sat muffled like the Fates; and often came
Melissa hitting all we saw with shafts
Of gentle satire, kin to charity,

That harm'd not: then day droopt; the chapel bells
Call'd us: we left the walks; we mixt with those
Six hundred maidens clad in purest white,
Before two streams of light from wall to wall,
While the great organ almost burst his pipes,
Groaning for power, and rolling thro' the court
A long melodious thunder to the sound
Of solemn psalms, and silver litanies,
The work of Ida, to call down from Heaven
A blessing on her labours for the world.

Sweet and low, sweet and low,
   Wind of the western sea,
Low, low, breathe and blow,
   Wind of the western sea!
Over the rolling waters go,
Come from the dying moon, and blow,
   Blow him again to me;
While my little one, while my pretty one, sleeps.

Sleep and rest, sleep and rest,
   Father will come to thee soon;
Rest, rest, on mother's breast,
   Father will come to thee soon;
Father will come to his babe in the nest,
Silver sails all out of the west
   Under the silver moon:
Sleep, my little one, sleep, my pretty one, sleep.

III.

Morn in the white wake of the morning star
Came furrowing all the orient into gold.
We rose, and each by other drest with care
Descended to the court that lay three parts
In shadow, but the Muses' heads were touch'd
Above the darkness from their native East.

There while we stood beside the fount, and watch'd
Or seem'd to watch the dancing bubble, approach'd
Melissa, tinged with wan from lack of sleep,
Or grief, and glowing round her dewy eyes
The circled Iris of a night of tears;
And "Fly" she cried, "O fly, while yet you may!
My mother knows:" and when I ask'd her "how"
"My fault" she wept "my fault! and yet not mine;
Yet mine in part.   O hear me, pardon me.
My mother, 'tis her wont from night to night
To rail at Lady Psyche and her side.
She says the Princess should have been the Head,
Herself and Lady Psyche the two arms;
And so it was agreed when first they came;
But Lady Psyche was the right hand now,
And she the left, or not, or seldom used;

14*

Hers more than half the students, all the love.
And so last night she fell to canvass you:
Her countrywomen! who did not envy her.
"Who ever saw such wild barbarians?
Girls? — more like men!" and at these words the snake,
My secret, seem'd to stir within my breast;
And oh, Sirs, could I help it, but my cheek
Began to burn and burn, and her lynx eye
To fix and make me hotter, till she laugh'd:
'O marvellously modest maiden, you!
Men! girls, like men! why, if they had been men
You need not set your thoughts in rubric thus
For wholesale comment.'   Pardon, I am shamed
That I must needs repeat for my excuse
What looks so little graceful: 'men' (for still
My mother went revolving on the word)
'And so they are, — very like men indeed —
And with that woman closeted for hours!"
Then came these dreadful words out one by one,
'Why — these — *are* — men:' I shudder'd: 'and you
            know it'
'O ask me nothing,' I said: 'And she knows too,
And she conceals it.'   So my mother clutch'd
The truth at once, but with no word from me;
And now thus early risen she goes to inform
The Princess: Lady Psyche will be crush'd;
But you may yet be saved, and therefore fly:
But heal me with your pardon ere you go."

.   "What pardon, sweet Melissa, for a blush?"
Said Cyril: "Pale one, blush again: than wear
Those lilies, better blush our lives away.
Yet let us breathe for one hour more in Heaven"
He added, "lest some classic Angel speak
In scorn of us, 'they mounted, Ganymedes,
To tumble, Vulcans, on the second morn,'
But I will melt this marble into wax
To yield us farther furlough:" and he went.

Melissa shook her doubtful curls, and thought
He scarce would prosper.   "Tell us," Florian ask'd,
"How grew this feud betwixt the right and left."
"O long ago," she said, "betwixt these two
Division smoulders hidden; 'tis my mother,
Too jealous, often fretful as the wind .
Pent in a crevice: much I bear with her:
I never knew my father, but she says
(God help her) she was wedded to a fool;
And still she rail'd against the state of things.
She had the care of Lady Ida's youth,
And from the Queen's decease she brought her up.
But when your sister came she won the heart
Of Ida: they were still together, grew
(For so they said themselves) inosculated;
Consonant chords that shiver to one note;
One mind in all things: yet my mother still
Affirms your Psyche thieved her theories,

And angled with them for her pupil's love:
She calls her plagiarist; I know not what:
But I must go: I dare not tarry" and light,
As flies the shadow of a bird, she fled.

Then murmur'd Florian gazing after her.
"An open-hearted maiden, true and pure.
If I could love, why this were she: how pretty
Her blushing was, and how she blush'd again,
As if to close with Cyril's random wish:
Not like your Princess cramm'd with erring pride,
Nor like poor Psyche whom she drags in tow."

"The crane," I said, "may chatter of the crane,
The dove may murmur of the dove, but I
An eagle clang an eagle to the sphere.
My princess, O my princess! true she errs,
But in her own grand way: being herself
Three times more noble than threescore of men,
She sees herself in every woman else,
And so she wears her error like a crown
To blind the truth and me: for her, and her,
Hebes are they to hand ambrosia, mix
The nectar; but — ah she — whene'er she moves
The Samian Herè rises and she speaks
A Memnon smitten with the morning Sun."

So saying from the court we paced, and gain'd
The terrace ranged along the Northern front,
And leaning there on those balusters, high
Above the empurpled champaign, drank the gale
That blown about the foliage underneath,
And sated with the innumerable rose,
Beat balm upon our eyelids.   Hither came
Cyril, and yawning "O hard task," he cried;
"No fighting shadows here!   I forced a way
Thro' solid opposition crabb'd and gnarl'd.
Better to clear prime forests, heave and thump
A league of street in summer solstice down,
Than hammer at this reverend gentlewoman.
I knock'd and, bidden, enter'd; found her there
At point to move, and settled in her eyes
The green malignant light of coming storm.
Sir, I was courteous, every phrase well-oil'd,
As man's could be; yet maiden-meek I pray'd
Concealment: she demanded who we were,
And why we came?   I fabled nothing fair,
But, your example pilot, told her all.
Up went the hush'd amaze of hand and eye.
But when I dwelt upon your old affiance,
She answer'd sharply that I talk'd astray.
I urged the fierce inscription on the gate,
And our three lives.   True — we had limed ourselves
With open eyes, and we must take the chance.
But such extremes, I told her, well might harm

The woman's cause. 'Not more than now,' she said,
'So puddled as it is with favouritism.'
I tried the mother's heart. Shame might befal
Melissa, knowing, saying not she knew:
Her answer was 'Leave me to deal with that.'
I spoke of war to come and many deaths,
And she replied, her duty was to speak,
And duty duty, clear of consequences.
I grew discouraged, Sir; but since I knew
No rock so hard but that a little wave
May beat admission in a thousand years,
I recommenced; 'Decide not ere you pause.
I find you here but in the second place,
Some say the third — the authentic foundress you.
I offer boldly: we will seat you highest:
Wink at our advent: help my prince to gain
His rightful bride, and here I promise you
Some palace in our land, where you shall reign
The head and heart of all our fair she-world,
And your great name flow on with broadening time
For ever.' Well, she balanced this a little,
And told me she would answer us to-day,
Meantime be mute: thus much, nor more I gain'd."

He ceasing, came a message from the Head.
"That afternoon the Princess rode to take
The dip of certain strata to the North.

Would we go with her? we should find the land
Worth seeing; and the river made a fall
Out yonder:" then she pointed on to where
A double hill ran up his furrowy forks
Beyond the thick-leaved platans of the vale.

Agreed to, this, the day fled on thro' all
Its range of duties to the appointed hour.
Then summon'd to the porch we went. She stood
Among her maidens, higher, by the head,
Her back against a pillar, her foot on one
Of those tame leopards. Kittenlike he roll'd
And paw'd about her sandal. I drew near;
I gazed. On a sudden my strange seizure came
Upon me, the weird vision of our house:
The Princess Ida seem'd a hollow show,
Her gay-furr'd cats a painted fantasy,
Her college and her maidens, empty masks,
And I myself the shadow of a dream,
For all things were and were not. Yet I felt
My heart beat thick with passion and with awe;
Then from my breast the involuntary sigh
Brake, as she smote me with the light of eyes
That lent my knee desire to kneel, and shook
My pulses, till to horse we got, and so
Went forth in long retinue following up
The river as it narrow'd to the hills.

I rode beside her and to me she said:
"O friend, we trust that you esteem'd us not
Too harsh to your companion yestermorn;
Unwillingly we spake."   "No — not to her,"
I answer'd, "but to one of whom we spake
Your Highness might have seem'd the thing you say."
"Again?" she cried "are you ambassadresses
From him to me? we give you, being strange,
A license: speak, and let the topic die."

I stammer'd that I knew him — could have wish'd —
"Our king expects — was there no precontract?
There is no truer-hearted — ah, you seem
All he prefigured, and he could not see
The bird of passage flying south but long'd
To follow: surely, if your Highness keep
Your purport, you will shock him ev'n to death,
Or baser courses, children of despair."

"Poor boy" she said "can he not read — no books?
Quoit, tennis, ball — no games? nor deals in that
Which men delight in, martial exercise?
To nurse a blind ideal like a girl,
Methinks he seems no better than a girl;
As girls were once, as we ourselves have been:
We had our dreams; perhaps he mixt with them:
We touch on our dead self, nor shun to do it,
Being other — since we learnt our meaning here,

To lift the woman's fall'n divinity
Upon an even pedestal with man."

She paused, and added with a haughtier smile
"And as to precontracts, we move, my friend,
At no man's beck, but know ourselves and thee,
O Vashti, noble Vashti! Summon'd out
She kept her state, and left the drunken king
To brawl at Shushan underneath the palms."

"Alas your Highness breathes full East," I said
"On that which leans to you. I know the Prince,
I prize his truth: and then how vast a work
To assail this gray preeminence of man!
You grant me license; might I use it? think;
Ere half be done perchance your life may fail;
Then comes the feebler heiress of your plan,
And takes and ruins all; and thus your pains
May only make that footprint upon sand
Which old-recurring waves of prejudice
Resmooth to nothing: might I dread that you,
With only Fame for spouse and your great deeds
For issue, yet may live in vain, and miss,
Meanwhile, what every woman counts her due,
Love, children, happiness?"
                              And she exclaim'd,
"Peace, you young savage of the Northern wild!
What! tho' your Prince's love were like a God's,

Have we not made ourself the sacrifice?
You are bold indeed: we are not talk'd to thus:
Yet will we say for children, would they grew
Like field-flowers everywhere! we like them well:
But children die; and let me tell you, girl,
Howe'er you babble, great deeds cannot die:
They with the sun and moon renew their light
For ever, blessing those that look on them.
Children — that men may pluck them from our hearts,
Kill us with pity, break us with ourselves —
O — children — there is nothing upon earth
More miserable than she that has a son
And sees him err: nor would we work for fame;
'Tho' she perhaps might reap the applause of Great,
Who learns the one $\pi o\upsilon\ \sigma\tau o$ whence after-hands
May move the world, tho' she herself effect
But little: wherefore up and act, nor shrink
For fear our solid aim be dissipated
By frail successors. Would, indeed, we had been,
In lieu of many mortal flies, a race
Of giants living, each, a thousand years,
That we might see our own work out, and watch
The sandy footprint harden into stone."

    I answer'd nothing, doubtful in myself
If that strange Poet-princess with her grand
Imaginations might at all be won.
And she broke out interpreting my thoughts:

"No doubt we seem a kind of monster to you;
We are used to that: for women, up till this
Cramp'd under worse than South-sea-isle taboo,
Dwarfs of the gynæceum, fail so far
In high desire, they know not, cannot guess
How much their welfare is a passion to us.
If we could give them surer, quicker proof —
Oh if our end were less achievable
By slow approaches, than by single act
Of immolation, any phase of death,
We were as prompt to spring against the pikes,
Or down the fiery gulf as talk of it,
To compass our dear sister's liberties."

She bow'd as if to veil a noble tear;
And up we came to where the river sloped
To plunge in cataract, shattering on black blocks
A breadth of thunder. O'er it shook the woods,
And danced the colour, and, below, stuck out
The bones of some vast bulk that lived and roar'd
Before man was. She gazed awhile and said,
"As these rude bones to us, are we to her
That will be." "Dare we dream of that," I ask'd,
"Which wronght us, as the workman and his work,
That practice betters?" "How," she cried, "you love
The metaphysics! read and earn our prize,
A golden broach: beneath an emerald plane
Sits Diotima, teaching him that died

Of hemlock; our device; wrought to the life;
She rapt upon her subject, he on her:
For there are schools for all."   "And yet" I said
"Methinks I have not found among them all
One anatomic."   "Nay, we thought of that,"
She answer'd, "but it pleased us not: in truth
We shudder but to dream our maids should ape
Those monstrous males that carve the living hound,
And cram him with the fragments of the grave,
Or in the dark dissolving human heart,
And holy secrets of this microcosm,
Dabbling a shameless hand with shameful jest,
Encarnalize their spirits: yet we know
Knowledge is knowledge, and this matter hangs:
Howbeit ourself, foreseeing casualty,
Nor willing men should come among us, learnt,
For many weary moons before we came,
This craft of healing.   Were you sick, ourself
Would tend upon you.   To your question now,
Which touches on the workman and his work.
Let there be light and there was light: 'tis so;
For was, and is, and will be, are but is;
And all creation is one act at once,
The birth of light: but we that are not all,
As parts, can see but parts, now this, now that,
And live, perforce, from thought to thought, and make
One act a phantom of succession: thus
Our weakness somehow shapes the shadow, Time;

But in the shadow will we work, and mould
The woman to the fuller day."

                            She spake
With kindled eyes: we rode a league beyond,
And, o'er a bridge of pinewood crossing, came
On flowery levels underneath the crag,
Full of all beauty. "O how sweet" I said
(For I was half-oblivious of my mask)
"To linger here with one that loved us." "Yea"
She answer'd "or with fair philosophics
That lift the fancy; for indeed these fields
Are lovely, lovelier not the Elysian lawns,
Where paced the Demigods of old, and saw
The soft white vapour streak the crowned towers
Built to the Sun:" then, turning to her maids,
"Pitch our pavilion here upon the sward;
Lay out the viands." At the word, they raised
A tent of satin, elaborately wrought
With fair Corinna's triumph; here she stood,
Engirt with many a florid maiden-cheek,
The woman-conqueror; woman-conquer'd there
The bearded Victor of ten-thousand hymns,
And all the men mourn'd at his side: but we
Set forth to climb; then, climbing, Cyril kept
With Psyche, with Melissa Florian, I
With mine affianced. Many a little hand
Glanced like a touch of sunshine on the rocks,
Many a light foot shone like a jewel set

In the dark crag: and then we turn'd, we wound
About the cliffs, the copses, out and in,
Hammering and clinking, chattering stony names
Of shale and hornblende, rag and trap and tuff,
Amygdaloid and trachyte, till the Sun
Grew broader toward his death and fell, and all
The rosy heights came out above the lawns.

The splendour falls on castle walls
　　And snowy summits old in story:
The long light shakes across the lakes,
　　And the wild cataract leaps in glory.
Blow, bugle, blow, set the wild echoes flying,
Blow, bugle; answer, echoes, dying, dying, dying.

O hark, O hear! how thin and clear,
　　And thinner, clearer, farther going!
O sweet and far from cliff and scar
　　The horns of Elfland faintly blowing!
Blow, let us hear the purple glens replying:
Blow, bugle; answer, echoes, dying, dying, dying.

O love, they die in yon rich sky,
　　They faint on hill or field or river:
Our echoes roll from soul to soul,
　　And grow for ever and for ever.
Blow, bugle, blow, set the wild echoes flying,
And answer, echoes, answer, dying, dying, dying.

IV.

"THERE sinks the nebulous star we call the Sun,
If that hypothesis of theirs be sound"
Said Ida; "let us down and rest;" and we
Down from the lean and wrinkled precipices,
By every coppice-feather'd chasm and cleft,
Dropt thro' the ambrosial gloom to where below
No bigger than a glow-worm shone the tent
Lamp-lit from the inner.   Once she lean'd on me,
Descending; once or twice she lent her hand,
And blissful palpitations in the blood,
Stirring a sudden transport rose and fell.

But when we planted level feet, and dipt
Beneath the satin dome and enter'd in,
There leaning deep in broider'd down we sank
Our elbows: on a tripod in the midst
A fragrant flame rose, and before us glow'd
Fruit, blossom, viand, amber wine, and gold.

Then she "Let some one sing to us: lightlier move
The minutes fledged with music:" and a maid,
Of those beside her, smote her harp, and sang.

"Tears, idle tears, I know not what they mean,
Tears from the depth of some divine despair
Rise in the heart, and gather to the eyes,
In looking on the happy Autumn-fields,
And thinking of the days that are no more.

"Fresh as the first beam glittering on a sail,
That brings our friends up from the underworld,
Sad as the last which reddens over one
That sinks with all we love below the verge;
So sad, so fresh, the days that are no more.

"Ah, sad and strange as in dark summer dawns
The earliest pipe of half-awaken'd birds
To dying ears, when unto dying eyes
The casement slowly grows a glimmering square;
So sad, so strange, the days that are no more.

"Dear as remember'd kisses after death,
And sweet as those by hopeless fancy feign'd
On lips that are for others; deep as love,
Deep as first love, and wild with all regret;
O Death in Life, the days that are no more."

She ended with such passion that the tear,
She sang of, shook and fell, an erring pearl
Lost in her bosom: but with some disdain
Answer'd the Princess "If indeed there haunt
15*

About the moulder'd lodges of the Past
So sweet a voice and vague, fatal to men,
Well needs it we should cram our ears with wool
And so pace by: but thine are fancies hatch'd
In silken-folded idleness; nor is it
Wiser to weep a true occasion lost,
But trim our sails, and let old bygones be,
While down the streams that float us each and all
To the issue, goes, like glittering bergs of ice,
Throne after throne, and molten on the waste
Becomes a cloud: for all things serve their time
Toward that great year of equal mights and rights,
Nor would I fight with iron laws, in the end
Found golden: let the past be past; let be
Their cancell'd Babels: tho' the rough kex break
The starr'd mosaic, and the wild goat hang
Upon the shaft, and the wild figtree split
Their monstrous idols, care not while we hear
A trumpet in the distance pealing news
Of better, and Hope, a poising eagle, burns
Above the unrisen morrow:" then to me;
"Know you no song of your own land," she said
"Not such as moans about the retrospect,
But deals with the other distance and the hues
Of promise; not a death's-head at the wine."

Then I remember'd one myself had made,
What time I watch'd the swallow winging south

From mine own land, part made long since, and part
Now while I sang, and maidenlike as far
As I could ape their treble, did I sing.

"O Swallow, Swallow, flying, flying South,
Fly to her, and fall upon her gilded eaves,
And tell her, tell her, what I tell to thee.

"O tell her, Swallow, thou that knowest each,
That bright and fierce and fickle is the South,
And dark and true and tender is the North.

"O Swallow, Swallow, if I could follow, and light
Upon her lattice, I would pipe and trill,
And cheep and twitter twenty million loves.

"O were I thou that she might take me in,
And lay me on her bosom, and her heart
Would rock the snowy cradle till I died.

"Why lingereth she to clothe her heart with love,
Delaying as the tender ash delays
To clothe herself, when all the woods are green?

"O tell her, Swallow, that thy brood is flown:
Say to her, I do but wanton in the South,
But in the North long since my nest is made.

"O tell her, brief is life but love is long,
And brief the sun of summer in the North,
And brief the moon of beauty in the South.

"O Swallow, flying from the golden woods,
Fly to her, and pipe and woo her, and make her mine,
And tell her, tell her, that I follow thee."

I ceased, and all the ladies, each at each,
Like the Ithacensian suitors in old time,
Stared with great eyes, and laugh'd with alien lips,
And knew not what they meant; for still my voice
Rang false: but smiling "Not for thee," she said,
"O Bulbul, any rose of Gulistan
Shall burst her veil: marsh-divers, rather, maid,
Shall croak thee sister, or the meadow-crake
Grate her harsh kindred in the grass: and this
A mere love-poem! O for such, my friend,
We hold them slight; they mind us of the time
When we made bricks in Egypt. Knaves are men,
That lute and flute fantastic tenderness,
And dress the victim to the offering up,
And paint the gates of Hell with Paradise,
And play the slave to gain the tyranny.
Poor soul! I had a maid of honour once;
She wept her true eyes blind for such a one,
A rogue of canzonets and serenades.

I loved her.   Peace be with her.   She is dead.
So they blaspheme the muse!   But great is song
Used to great ends: ourself have often tried
Valkyrian hymns, or into rhythm have dash'd
The passion of the prophetess; for song
Is duer unto freedom, force and growth
Of spirit than to junketing and love.
Love is it?   Would this same mock-love, and this
Mock-Hymen were laid up like winter bats,
Till all men grew to rate us at our worth,
Not vassals to be beat, nor pretty babes
To be dandled, no, but living wills, and sphered
Whole in ourselves and owed to none.   Enough!
But now to leaven play with profit, you,
Know you no song, the true growth of your soil,
That gives the manners of your countrywomen?"

        She spoke and turn'd her sumptuous head with eyes
Of shining expectation fixt on mine.
Then while I dragg'd my brains for such a song,
Cyril, with whom the bell-mouth'd flask had wrought,
Or master'd by the sense of sport, began
To troll a careless, careless tavern-catch
Of Moll and Meg, and strange experiences
Unmeet for ladies.   Florian nodded at him,
I frowning; Psyche flush'd and wann'd and shook;
The lilylike Melissa droop'd her brows;

"Forbear" the Princess cried; "Forbear, Sir" I;
And heated thro' and thro' with wrath and love,
I smote him on the breast; he started up;
There rose a shriek as of a city sack'd;
Melissa clamour'd "Flee the death;" "To horse"
Said Ida; "home! to horse!" and fled, as flies
A troop of snowy doves athwart the dusk,
When some one batters at the dovecote-doors,
Disorderly the women. Alone I stood
With Florian, cursing Cyril, vext at heart,
In the pavilion: there like parting hopes
I heard them passing from me: hoof by hoof,
And every hoof a knell to my desires,
Clang'd on the bridge; and then another shriek,
"The Head, the Head, the Princess, O the Head!"
For blind with rage she miss'd the plank, and roll'd
In the river. Out I sprang from glow to gloom:
There whirl'd her white robe like a blossom'd branch
Rapt to the horrible fall: a glance I gave,
No more; but woman-vested as I was
Plunged; and the flood drew; yet I caught her; then
Oaring one arm, and bearing in my left
The weight of all the hopes of half the world,
Strove to buffet to land in vain. A tree
Was half-disrooted from his place and stoop'd
To drench his dark locks in the gurgling wave
Mid-channel. Right on this we drove and caught,
And grasping down the boughs I gain'd the shore.

There stood her maidens glimmeringly group'd
In the hollow bank.   One reaching forward drew
My burthen from mine arms; they cried "she lives!"
They bore her back into the tent: but I,
So much a kind of shame within me wrought,
Not yet endured to meet her opening. eyes,
Nor found my friends: but push'd alone on foot
(For since her horse was lost I left her mine)
Across the woods, and less from Indian craft
Than beelike instinct hiveward, found at length
The garden portals.   Two great statues, Art
And Science, Caryatids, lifted up
A weight of emblem, and betwixt were valves
Of open-work in which the hunter rued
His rash intrusion, manlike, but his brows
Had sprouted, and the branches thereupon
Spread out at top, and grimly spiked the gates.

A little space was left between the horns,
Thro' which I clamber'd o'er at top with pain,
Dropt on the sward, and up the linden walks,
And, tost on thoughts that changed from hue to hue,
Now poring on the glowworm, now the star,
I paced the terrace, till the bear had wheel'd
'Thro' a great arc his seven slow suns.

                                        A step
Of lightest echo, then a loftier form
Than female, moving thro' the uncertain gloom,

Disturb'd me with the doubt "if this were she"
But it was Florian.   "Hist O hist," he said,
"They seek us: out so late is out of rules.
Moreover 'seize the strangers' is the cry.
How came you here," I told him: "I" said he,
"Last of the train, a moral leper, I,
To whom none spake, half-sick at heart, return'd.
Arriving all confused among the rest
With hooded brows I crept into the hall,
And, couch'd behind a Judith, underneath
The head of Holofernes peep'd and saw.
Girl after girl was call'd to trial: each
Disclaim'd all knowledge of us: last of all,
Melissa: trust me, Sir, I pitied her.
She, question'd if she knew us men, at first
Was silent; closer prest, denied it not:
And then, demanded if her mother knew,
Or Psyche, she affirm'd not, or denied:
From whence the Royal mind, familiar with her,
Easily gather'd either guilt.   She sent
For Psyche, but she was not there; she call'd
For Psyche's child to cast it from the doors:
She sent for Blanche to accuse her face to face;
And I slipt out: but whither will you now?
And where are Psyche, Cyril? both are fled:
What, if together? that were not so well.
Would rather we had never come! I dread
His wildness, and the chances of the dark."

"And yet," I said, "you wrong him more than I
That struck him: this is proper to the clown,
Tho' smock'd, or furr'd and purpled, still the clown,
To harm the thing that trusts him, and to shame
That which he says he loves: for Cyril, howe'er
He deal in frolic, as to-night — the song
Might have been worse and sinn'd in grosser lips
Beyond all pardon — as it is, I hold
These flashes on the surface are not he.
He has a solid base of temperament:
But as the waterlily starts and slides
Upon the level in little puffs of wind,
Tho' anchor'd to the bottom, such is he."

Scarce had I ceased when from a tamarisk near
Two Proctors leapt upon us, crying, "Names:"
He, standing still, was clutch'd; but I began
To thrid the musky-circled mazes, wind
And double in and out the boles, and race
By all the fountains: fleet I was of foot:
Before me shower'd the rose in flakes; behind
I heard the puff'd pursuer; at mine ear
Bubbled the nightingale and heeded not,
And secret laughter tickled all my soul.
At last I hook'd my ancle in a vine,
That claspt the feet of a Mnemosyne,
And falling on my face was caught and known.

They haled us to the Princess where she sat
High in the hall: above her droop'd a lamp,
And made the single jewel on her brow
Burn like the mystic fire on a mast-head,
Prophet of storm: a handmaid on each side
Bow'd toward her, combing out her long black hair
Damp from the river; and close behind her stood
Eight daughters of the plough, stronger than men,
Huge women blowzed with health, and wind, and rain,
And labour. Each was like a Druid rock;
Or like a spire of land that stands apart
Cleft from the main, and wail'd about with mews.

Then, as we came, the crowd dividing clove
An advent to the throne; and therebeside,
Half-naked as if caught at once from bed
And tumbled on the purple footcloth, lay
The lily-shining child; and on the left,
Bow'd on her palms and folded up from wrong,
Her round white shoulder shaken with her sobs,
Melissa knelt; but Lady Blanche erect
Stood up and spake, an affluent orator.

"It was not thus, O Princess, in old days:
You prized my counsel, lived upon my lips:
I led you then to all the Castalies;
I fed you with the milk of every Muse;
I loved you like this kneeler, and you me

Your second mother: those were gracious times.
Then came your new friend: you began to change —
I saw it and grieved — to slacken and to cool;
Till taken with her seeming openness
You turn'd your warmer currents all to her,
To me you froze: this was my meed for all.
Yet I bore up in part from ancient love,
And partly that I hoped to win you back,
And partly conscious of my own deserts,
And partly that you were my civil head,
And chiefly you were born for something great,
In which I might your fellow-worker be,
When time should serve; and thus a noble scheme
Grew up from seed we two long since had sown;
In us true growth, in her a Jonah's gourd,
Up in one night and due to sudden sun:
We took this palace; but even from the first
You stood in your own light and darken'd mine.
What student came but that you planed her path
To Lady Psyche, younger, not so wise,
A foreigner, and I your countrywoman,
I your old friend and tried, she new in all?
But still her lists were swell'd and mine were lean;
Yet I bore up in hope she would be known:
Then came these wolves: *they* knew her: *they* endured,
Long-closeted with her the yestermorn,
To tell her what they were, and she to hear:
And me none told: not less to an eye like mine,

A lidless watcher of the public weal,
Last night, their mask was patent, and my foot
Was to you: but I thought again: I fear'd
To meet a cold 'We thank you, we shall hear of it
From Lady Psyche:' you had gone to her,
She told, perforce; and winning easy grace,
No doubt, for slight delay, remain'd among us
In our young nursery still unknown, the stem
Less grain than touchwood, while my honest heat
Were all miscounted as malignant haste
To push my rival out of place and power.
But public use required she should be known;
And since my oath was ta'en for public use,
I broke the letter of it to keep the sense.
I spoke not then at first, but watch'd them well,
Saw that they kept apart, no mischief done;
And yet this day (tho' you should hate me for it)
I came to tell you; found that you had gone,
Ridd'n to the hills, she likewise: now, I thought,
That surely she will speak; if not, then I:
Did she? These monsters blazon'd what they were,
According to the coarseness of their kind,
For thus I hear; and known at last (my work)
And full of cowardice and guilty shame,
I grant in her some sense of shame, she flies;
And I remain on whom to wreak your rage,
I, that have lent my life to build up yours,
I that have wasted here health, wealth, and time,

And talents, I — you know it — I will not boast:
Dismiss me, and I prophesy your plan,
Divorced from my experience, will be chaff
For every gust of chance, and men will say
We did not know the real light, but chased
The wisp that flickers where no foot can tread."

Sho ceased: the Princess answer'd coldly "Good:
Your oath is broken: we dismiss you: go.
For this lost lamb (she pointed to the child)
Our mind is changed: we take it to ourselves."

Thereat the Lady stretch'd a vulture throat,
And shot from crooked lips a haggard smile.
"The plan was mine. I built the nest" she said
"To hatch the cuckoo. Rise!" and stoop'd to updrag
Melissa: she, half on her mother propt,
Half-drooping from her, turn'd her face, and cast
A liquid look on Ida, full of prayer,
Which melted Florian's fancy as she hung,
A Niobëan daughter, one arm out,
Appealing to the bolts of Heaven; and while
We gazed upon her came a little stir
About the doors, and on a sudden rush'd
Among us, out of breath, as one pursued,
A woman-post in flying raiment. Fear
Stared in her eyes, and chalk'd her face, and wing'd
Her transit to the throne, whereby she fell

Delivering seal'd dispatches which the Head
Took half-amazed, and in her lion's mood
Tore open, silent we with blind surmise
Regarding, while she read, till over brow
And cheek and bosom brake the wrathful bloom
As of some fire against a stormy cloud,
When the wild peasant rights himself, the rick
Flames, and his anger reddens in the heavens;
For anger most it seem'd, while now her breast,
Beaten with some great passion at her heart,
Palpitated, her hand shook, and we heard
In the dead hush the papers that she held
Rustle: at once the lost lamb at her feet
Sent out a bitter bleating for its dam;
The plaintive cry jarr'd on her ire; she crush'd
The scrolls together, made a sudden turn
As if to speak, but, utterance failing her,
She whirl'd them on to me, as who should say
"Read" and I read — two letters — one her sire's.

    "Fair daughter, when we sent the Prince your way
We know not your ungracious laws, which learnt,
We, conscious of what temper you are built,
Came all in haste to hinder wrong, but fell
Into his father's hands, who has this night,
You lying close upon his territory,
Slipt round and in the dark invested you,
And here he keeps me hostage for his son."

The second was my father's running thus:
"You have our son: touch not a hair of his head:
Render him up unscathed: give him your hand:
Cleave to your contract: tho' indeed we hear
You hold the woman is the better man;
A rampant heresy, such as if it spread
Would make all women kick against their Lords
Thro' all the world, and which might well deserve
That we this night should pluck your palace down;
And we will do it, unless you send us back
Our son, on the instant, whole."

                So far I read;
And then stood up and spoke impetuously.

"O not to pry and peer on your reserve,
But led by golden wishes, and a hope
The child of regal compact, did I break
Your precinct; not a scorner of your sex
But venerator, zealous it should be
All that it might be: hear me, for I bear,
Tho' man, yet human, whatsoe'er your wrongs,
From the flaxen curl to the gray lock a life
Less mine than yours: my nurse would tell me of you;
I babbled for you, as babies for the moon,
Vague brightness; when a boy, you stoop'd to me
From all high places, lived in all fair lights,
Came in long breezes rapt from inmost south
And blown to inmost north; at eve and dawn

With Ida, Ida, Ida, rang the woods;
The leader wildswan in among the stars
Would clang it, and lapt in wreaths of glowworm light
The mellow breaker murmur'd Ida. Now,
Because I would have reach'd you, had you been
Sphered up with Cassiopëia, or the enthroned
Persephone in Hades, now at length,
Those winters of abeyance all worn out,
A man I came to see you: but, indeed,
Not in this frequence can I lend full tongue,
O noble Ida, to those thoughts that wait
On you, their centre: let me say but this,
That many a famous man and woman, town
And landskip, have I heard of, after seen
The dwarfs of presage; tho' when known, there grew
Another kind of beauty in detail
Made them worth knowing; but in you I found
My boyish dream involved and dazzled down
And master'd, while that after-beauty makes
Such head from act to act, from hour to hour,
Within me, that except you slay me here,
According to your bitter statute-book,
I cannot cease to follow you, as they say
The seal does music; who desire you more
Than growing boys their manhood; dying lips,
With many thousand matters left to do,
The breath of life; O more than poor men wealth,
Than sick men health — yours, yours, not mine — but half

Without you; with you, whole; and of those halves
You worthiest; and howe'er you block and bar
Your heart with system out from mine, I hold
That it becomes no man to nurse despair,
But in the teeth of clench'd antagonisms
To follow up the worthiest till he die:
Yet that I came not all unauthorized
Behold your father's letter."

      On one knee
Kneeling, I gave it, which she caught, and dash'd
Unopen'd at her feet: a tide of fierce
Invective seem'd to wait behind her lips,
As waits a river level with the dam
Ready to burst and flood the world with foam:
And so she would have spoken, but there rose
A hubbub in the court of half the maids
Gather'd together: from the illumined hall
Long lanes of splendour slanted o'er a press
Of snowy shoulders, thick as herded ewes,
And rainbow robes, and gems and gemlike eyes,
And gold and golden heads; they to and fro
Fluctuated, as flowers in storm, some red, some pale,
All open-mouth'd, all gazing to the light,
Some crying there was an army in the land,
And some that men were in the very walls,
And some they cared not; till a clamour grew
As of a new-world Babel, woman-built,

        16.*

And worse-confounded: high above them stood
The placid marble Muses, looking peace.

    Not peace she look'd, the Head: but rising up
Robed in the long night of her deep hair, so
To the open window moved, remaining there
Fixt like a beacon-tower above the waves
Of tempest, when the crimson-rolling eye
Glares ruin, and the wild birds on the light
Dash themselves dead. She stretch'd her arms and call'd
Across the tumult and the tumult fell.

    "What fear ye brawlers? am not I your Head?
On me, me, me, the storm first breaks: *I* dare
All these male thunderbolts: what is it ye fear?
Peace! there are those to avenge us and they come:
If not, — myself were like enough, O girls,
To unfurl the maiden banner of our rights,
And clad in iron burst the ranks of war,
Or, falling, protomartyr of our cause,
Die: yet I blame ye not so much for fear;
Six thousand years of fear have made ye that
From which I would redeem ye: but for those
That stir this hubbub — you and you — I know
Your faces there in the crowd — to-morrow morn
We hold a great convention: then shall they
That love their voices more than duty, learn

With whom they deal, dismiss'd in shame to live
No wiser than their mothers, household stuff,
Live chattels, mincers of each other's fame,
Full of weak poison, turnspits for the clown,
The drunkard's football, laughing-stocks of Time,
Whose brains are in their hands and in their heels,
But fit to flaunt, to dress, to dance, to thrum,
To tramp, to scream, to burnish, and to scour,
For ever slaves at home and fools abroad."

    She, ending, waved her hands: thereat the crowd
Muttering, dissolved: then with a smile, that look'd
A stroke of cruel sunshine on the cliff,
When all the glens are drown'd in azure gloom
Of thunder-shower, she floated to us and said:

    "You have done well and like a gentleman,
And like a prince: you have our thanks for all:
And you look well too in your woman's dress:
Well have you done and like a gentleman.
You saved our life: we owe you bitter thanks:
Better have died and spilt our bones in the flood —
Then men had said — but now — What hinders me
To take such bloody vengeance on you both? —
Yet since our father — Wasps in our good hive,
You would-be quenchers of the light to be,
Barbarians, grosser than your native bears —
O would I had his sceptre for one hour!

You that have dared to break our bound, and gull'd
Our servants, wrong'd and lied and thwarted us —
I wed with thee! *I* bound by precontract
Your bride, your bondslave! not tho' all the gold
That veins the world were pack'd to make your crown,
And every spoken tongue should lord you.　Sir,
Your falsehood and yourself are hateful to us:
I trample on your offers and on you:
Begone: we will not look upon you more.
Here, push them out at gates."

In wrath she spake.

Then those eight mighty daughters of the plough
Bent their broad faces toward us and address'd
Their motion: twice I sought to plead my cause,
But on my shoulder hung their heavy hands,
The weight of destiny: so from her face
They push'd us, down the steps, and thro' the court,
And with grim laughter thrust us out at gates.

We cross'd the street and gain'd a petty mound
Beyond it, whence we saw the lights and heard
The voices murmuring.　While I listen'd, came
On a sudden the weird seizure and the doubt:
I seem'd to move among a world of ghosts;
The Princess with her monstrous woman-guard,
The jest and earnest working side by side,
The cataract and the tumult and the kings
Were shadows; and the long fantastic night

With all its doings had and had not been,
And all things were and were not.

         This went by
As strangely as it came, and on my spirits
Settled a gentle cloud of melancholy;
Not long; I shook it off; for spite of doubts
And sudden ghostly shadowings I was one
To whom the touch of all mischance but came
As night to him that sitting on a hill
Sees the midsummer, midnight, Norway sun
Set into sunrise; then we moved away.

Thy voice is heard thro' rolling drums,
  That beat to battle where he stands;
Thy face across his fancy comes,
  And gives the battle to his hands:
A moment, while the trumpets blow,
  He sees his brood about thy knee;
The next, like fire he meets the foe,
  And strikes him dead for thine and thee.

So Lilia sang: we thought her half-possess'd,
She struck such warbling fury thro' the words;
And, after, feigning pique at what she call'd
The raillery, or grotesque, or false sublime —
Like one that wishes at a dance to change
The music — clapt her hands and cried for war,
Or some grand fight to kill and make an end:
And he that next inherited the tale
Half turning to the broken statue, said,
"Sir Ralph has got your colours: if I prove
Your knight, and fight your battle, what for me?"
It chanced, her empty glove upon the tomb
Lay by her like a model of her hand.
She took it and she flung it. "Fight" she said,
"And make us all we would be, great and good."
He knightlike in his cap instead of casque,
A cap of Tyrol borrow'd from the hall,
Arranged the favour, and assumed the Prince.

V.

Now, scarce three paces measured from the mound,
We stumbled on a stationary voice,
And "Stand, who goes?" "Two from the palace" I.
"The second two: they wait," he said, "pass on;
His Highness wakes:" and one, that clash'd in arms,
By glimmering lanes and walls of canvas, led
Threading the soldier-city, till we heard
The drowsy folds of our great ensign shake
From blazon'd lions o'er the imperial tent
Whispers of war.
　　　　　　　Entering, the sudden light
Dazed me half-blind: I stood and seem'd to hear,
As in a poplar grove when a light wind wakes
A lisping of the innumerous leaf and dies,
Each hissing in his neighbour's ear; and then
A strangled titter, out of which there brake
On all sides, clamouring etiquette to death
Unmeasured mirth; while now the two old kings
Began to wag their baldness up and down,
The fresh young captains flash'd their glittering teeth,
The huge bush-bearded Barons heaved and blew,
And slain with laughter roll'd the gilded Squire.

At length my Sire, his rough cheek wet with tears,
Panted from weary sides "King, you are free!
We did but keep you surely for our son,
If this be he, — or a draggled mawkin, thou,
That tends her bristled grunters in the sludge:"
For I was drench'd with ooze, and torn with briers,
More crumpled than a poppy from the sheath,
And all one rag, disprinced from head to heel.
Then some one sent beneath his vaulted palm
A whisper'd jest to some one near him "Look,
He has been among his shadows." "Satan take
The old women and their shadows! (thus the King
Roar'd) make yourself a man to fight with men.
Go: Cyril told us all."

                As boys that slink
From ferule and the trespass-chiding eye,
Away we stole, and transient in a trice
From what was left of faded woman-slough
To sheathing splendours and the golden scale
Of harness, issued in the sun, that now
Leapt from the dewy shoulders of the Earth,
And hit the northern hills. Here Cyril met us,
A little shy at first, but by and by
We twain, with mutual pardon ask'd and given
For stroke and song, resolder'd peace, whereon
Follow'd his tale. Amazed he fled away
Thro' the dark land, and later in the night
Had come on Psyche weeping: "then we fell

Into your father's hand, and there she lies,
But will not speak, nor stir."
                                      He show'd a tent
A stone-shot off: we enter'd in, and there
Among piled arms and rough accoutrements,
Pitiful sight, wrapp'd in a soldier's cloak,
Like some sweet sculpture draped from head to foot,
And push'd by rude hands from its pedestal,
All her fair length upon the ground she lay:
And at her head a follower of the camp,
A charr'd and wrinkled piece of womanhood,
Sat watching like a watcher by the dead.

Then Florian knelt, and "Come" he whisper'd to her
"Lift up your head, sweet sister: lie not thus.
What have you done but right? you could not slay
Me, nor your prince: look up: be comforted:
Sweet is it to have done the thing one ought,
When fall'n in darker ways." And likewise I:
"Be comforted: have I not lost her too,
In whose least act abides the nameless charm
That none has else for me?" She heard, she moved,
She moan'd, a folded voice; and up she sat,
And raised the cloak from brows as pale and smooth
As those that mourn half-shrouded over death
In deathless marble. "Her" she said "my friend —
Parted from her — betray'd her cause and mine —
Where shall I breathe? why kept ye not your faith?

O base and bad! what comfort? none for me!"
To whom remorseful Cyril "Yet I pray
Take comfort: live, dear lady, for your child!"
At which she lifted up her voice and cried.

  "Ah me, my babe, my blossom, ah my child,
My one sweet child, whom I shall see no more!
For now will cruel Ida keep her back;
And either she will die from want of care,
Or sicken with ill usage, when they say
The child is hers — for every little fault,
The child is hers; and they will beat my girl
Remembering her mother: O my flower!
Or they will take her, they will make her hard,
And she will pass me by in after-life
With some cold reverence worse than were she dead.
Ill mother that I was to leave her there,
To lag behind, scared by the cry they made,
The horror of the shame among them all:
But I will go and sit beside the doors,
And make a wild petition night and day,
Until they hate to hear me like a wind
Wailing for ever, till they open to me,
And lay my little blossom at my feet,
My babe, my sweet Aglaïa, my one child:
And I will take her up and go my way,
And satisfy my soul with kissing her:
Ah! what might that man not deserve of me,

Who gave me back my child?" "Be comforted"
Said Cyril "you shall have it:" but again
She veil'd her brows, and prone she sank, and so
Like tender things that being caught feign death,
Spoke not, nor stirr'd.

     By this a murmur ran
Thro' all the camp and inward raced the scouts
With rumour of Prince Arac hard at hand.
We left her by the woman, and without
Found the gray kings at parle; and "Look you" cried
My father "that our compact be fulfill'd:
You have spoilt this child; she laughs at you and man:
She wrongs herself, her sex, and me, and him:
But red-faced war has rods of steel and fire;
She yields, or war."

     Then Gama turn'd to me:
"We fear, indeed, you spent a stormy time
With our strange girl: and yet they say that still
You love her. Give us, then, your mind at large:
How say you, war or not?"

       "Not war, if possible,
O king," I said, "lest from the abuse of war,
The desecrated shrine, the trampled year,
The smouldering homestead, and the household flower
Torn from the lintel — all the common wrong —
A smoke go up thro' which I loom to her
Three times a monster: now she lightens scorn
At him that mars her plan, but then would hate

(And every voice she talk'd with ratify it,
And every face she look'd on justify it)
The general foe.   More soluble is this knot,
By gentleness than war.   I want her love.
What were I nigher this altho' we dash'd
Your cities into shards with catapults,
She would not love;—or brought her chain'd, a slave,
The lifting of whose eyelash is my lord,
Not ever would she love; but brooding turn
The book of scorn, till all my little chance
Were caught within the record of her wrongs,
And crush'd to death: and rather, Sire, than this
I would the old God of war himself were dead,
Forgotten, rusting on his iron hills,
Rotting on some wild shore with ribs of wreck,
Or like an old-world mammoth bulk'd in ice,
Not to be molten out."

                    And roughly spake
My father, "Tut, you know them not, the girls.
Boy, when I hear you prate I almost think
That idiot legend credible.   Look you, Sir!
Man is the hunter; woman is his game:
The sleek and shining creatures of the chase,
We hunt them for the beauty of their skins;
They love us for it, and we ride them down.
Wheedling and siding with them!   Out! for shame!
Boy, there's no rose that's half so dear to them
As he that does the thing they dare not do,

Breathing and sounding beauteous battle, comes
With the air of the trumpet round him, and leaps in
Among the women, snares them by the score
Flatter'd and fluster'd, wins, tho' dash'd with death
He reddens what he kisses: thus I won
Your mother, a good mother, a good wife,
Worth winning; but this firebrand — gentleness
To such as her! if Cyril spake her true,
To catch a dragon in a cherry net,
To trip a tigress with a gossamer,
Were wisdom to it."

     "Yea but Sire," I cried,
"Wild natures need wise curbs. The soldier?   No:
What dares not Ida do that she should prize
The soldier?   I beheld her, when she rose
The yesternight, and storming in extremes
Stood for her cause, and flung defiance down
Gagelike to man, and had not shunn'd the death,
No, not the soldier's: yet I hold her, king,
True woman: but you clash them all in one,
That have as many differences as we.
The violet varies from the lily as far
As oak from elm: one loves the soldier, one
The silken priest of peace, one this, one that,
And some unworthily; their sinless faith,
A maiden moon that sparkles on a sty,
Glorifying clown and satyr; whence they need
More breadth of culture: is not Ida right?

They worth it? truer to the law within?
Severer in the logic of a life?
Twice as magnetic to sweet influences
Of earth and heaven? and she of whom you speak,
My mother, looks as whole as some serene
Creation minted in the golden moods
Of sovereign artists; not a thought, a touch,
But pure as lines of green that streak the white
Of the first snowdrop's inner leaves; I say,
Not like the piebald miscellany, man,
Bursts of great heart and slips in sensual mire,
But whole and one: and take them all-in-all,
Were we ourselves but half as good, as kind,
As truthful, much that Ida claims as right
Had ne'er been mooted, but as frankly theirs
As dues of Nature.   To our point: not war:
Lest I lose all."

                  "Nay, nay, you spake but sense"
Said Gama.   "We remember love ourselves
In our sweet youth; we did not rate him then
This red-hot iron to be shaped with blows.
You talk almost like Ida: *she* can talk;
And there is something in it as you say:
But you talk kindlier: we esteem you for it. —
He seems a gracious and a gallant Prince,
I would he had our daughter: for the rest,
Our own detention, why, the causes weigh'd,
Fatherly fears — you used us courteously —

We would do much to gratify your Prince —
We pardon it; and for your ingress here
Upon the skirt and fringe of our fair land,
You did but come as goblins in the night,
Nor in the furrow broke the ploughman's head,
Nor burnt the grange, nor buss'd the milking-maid,
Nor robb'd the farmer of his bowl of cream:
But let your Prince (our royal word upon it,
He comes back safe) ride with us to our lines,
And speak with Arac: Arac's word is thrice
As ours with Ida: something may be done —
I know not what — and ours shall see us friends.
You, likewise, our late guests, if so you will,
Follow us: who knows? we four may build some plan
Foursquare to opposition."

                        Here he reach'd
White hands of farewell to my sire, who growl'd
An answer which, half-muffled in his beard,
Let so much out as gave us leave to go.

    Then rode we with the old king across the lawns
Beneath huge trees, a thousand rings of Spring
In every bole, a song on every spray
Of birds that piped their Valentines, and woke
Desire in me to infuse my tale of love
In the old king's ears, who promised help, and oozed
All o'er with honey'd answer as we rode;
And blossom-fragrant slipt the heavy dews

Gather'd by night and peace, with each light air
On our mail'd heads: but other thoughts than Peace
Burnt in us, when we saw the embattled squares,
And squadrons of the Prince, trampling the flowers
With clamour: for among them rose a cry
As if to greet the king; they made a halt;
The horses yell'd; they clash'd their arms; the drum
Beat; merrily-blowing shrill'd the martial fife;
And in the blast and bray of the long horn
And serpent-throated bugle, undulated
The banner: anon to meet us lightly pranced
Three captains out; nor ever had I seen
Such thews of men: the midmost and the highest
Was Arac: all about his motion clung
The shadow of his sister, as the beam
Of the East, that play'd upon them, made them glance
Like those three stars of the airy Giant's zone,
That glitter burnish'd by the frosty dark;
And as the fiery Sirius alters hue,
And bickers into red and emerald, shone
Their morions, wash'd with morning, as they came.

And I that prated peace, when first I heard
War-music, felt the blind wildbeast of force,
Whose home is in the sinews of a man,
Stir in me as to strike: then took the king
His three broad sons; with now a wandering hand
And now a pointed finger, told them all:

A common light of smiles at our disguise
Broke from their lips, and, ere the windy jest
Had labour'd down within his ample lungs,
The genial giant, Arac, roll'd himself
Thrice in the saddle, then burst out in words.

"Our land invaded, 'sdeath! and he himself
Your captive, yet my father wills not war:
And, 'sdeath! myself, what care I, war or no?
But then this question of your troth remains:
And there's a downright honest meaning in her;
She flies too high, she flies too high! and yet
She ask'd but space and fairplay for her scheme;
She prest and prest it on me — I myself,
What know I of these things? but, life and soul!
I thought her half-right talking of her wrongs;
I say she flies too high, 'sdeath! what of that?
I take her for the flower of womankind,
And so I often told her, right or wrong,
And, Prince, she can be sweet to those she loves,
And, right or wrong, I care not: this is all,
I stand upon her side: she made me swear it —
'Sdeath — and with solemn rites by candle-light —
Swear by St. something — I forget her name —
Her that talk'd down the fifty wisest men;
She was a princess too; and so I swore.
Come, this is all; she will not: waive your claim:

If not, the foughten field, what else, at once
Decides it, 'sdeath! against my father's will."

    I lagg'd in answer loth to render up
My precontract, and loth by brainless war
To cleave the rift of difference deeper yet;
Till one of those two brothers, half aside
And fingering at the hair about his lip,
To prick us on to combat "Like to like!
The woman's garment hid the woman's heart."
A taunt that clench'd his purpose like a blow!
For fiery-short was Cyril's counter-scoff,
And sharp I answer'd, touch'd upon the point
Where idle boys are cowards to their shame,
"Decide it here: why not? we are three to three."

    Then spake the third "But three to three? no more?
No more, and in our noble sister's cause?
More, more, for honour: every captain waits
Hungry for honour, angry for his king.
More, more, some fifty on a side, that each
May breathe himself, and quick! by overthrow
Of these or those, the question settled die."

    "Yea" answer'd I "for this wild wreath of air,
This flake of rainbow flying on the highest
Foam of men's deeds — this honour, if ye will
It needs must be for honour if at all:

Since, what decision? if we fail, we fail,
And if we win, we fail: she would not keep
Her compact."   "'Sdeath! but we will send to her,"
Said Arac, "worthy reasons why she should
Bide by this issue: let our missive thro',
And you shall have her answer by the word."

    "Boys!" shrieked the old king, but vainlier than a hen
To her false daughters in the pool; for none
Regarded; neither seem'd there more to say:
Back rode we to my father's camp, and found
He thrice had sent a herald to the gates,
To learn if Ida yet would cede our claim,
Or by denial flush her babbling wells
With her own people's life: three times he went:
The first, he blew and blew, but none appear'd:
He batter'd at the doors; none came: the next,
An awful voice within had warn'd him thence:
The third, and those eight daughters of the plough
Came sallying thro' the gates, and caught his hair,
And so belabour'd him on rib and cheek
They made him wild: not less one glance he caught
Thro' open doors of Ida station'd there
Unshaken, clinging to her purpose, firm
Tho' compass'd by two armies and the noise
Of arms; and standing like a stately Pine
Set in a cataract on an island-crag,

When storm is on the heights, and right and left
Suck'd from the dark heart of the long hills roll
The torrents, dash'd to the vale: and yet her will
Bred will in me to overcome it or fall.

But when I told the king that I was pledged
To fight in tourney for my bride, he clash'd
His iron palms together with a cry;
Himself would tilt it out among the lads:
But overborne by all his bearded lords
With reasons drawn from age and state, perforce
He yielded, wroth and red, with fierce demur:
And many a bold knight started up in heat,
And sware to combat for my claim till death.

All on this side the palace ran the field
Flat to the garden-wall: and likewise here,
Above the garden's glowing blossom-belts,
A column'd entry shone and marble stairs,
And great bronze valves, emboss'd with Tomyris
And what she did to Cyrus after fight,
But now fast barr'd: so here upon the flat
All that long morn the lists were hammer'd up,
And all that morn the heralds to and fro,
With message and defiance, went and came;
Last, Ida's answer, in a royal hand,
But shaken here and there, and rolling words
Oration-like.   I kiss'd it and I read.

"O brother, you have known the pangs we felt,
What heats of indignation when we heard
Of those that iron-cramp'd their women's feet;
Of lands in which at the altar the poor bride
Gives her harsh groom for bridal-gift a scourge;
Of living hearts that crack within the fire
Where smoulder their dead despots; and of those, —
Mothers, — that, all prophetic pity, fling
Their pretty maids in the running flood, and swoops
The vulture, beak and talon, at the heart
Made for all noble motion: and I saw
That equal baseness lived in sleeker times
With smoother men: the old leaven leaven'd all:
Millions of throats would bawl for civil rights,
No woman named: therefore I set my face
Against all men, and lived but for mine own.
Far off from men I built a fold for them:
I stored it full of rich memorial:
I fenced it round with gallant institutes,
And biting laws to scare the beasts of prey,
And prosper'd; till a rout of saucy boys
Brake on us at our books, and marr'd our peace,
Mask'd like our maids, blustering I know not what
Of insolence and love, some pretext held
Of baby troth, invalid, since my will
Seal'd not the bond — the striplings! — for their sport! —
I tamed my leopards: shall I not tame these?
Or you? or I? for since you think me touch'd

In honour — what, I would not aught of false —
Is not our cause pure? and whereas I know
Your prowess, Arac, and what mother's blood
You draw from, fight; you failing, I abide
What end soever: fail you will not.   Still
Take not his life: he risk'd it for my own;
His mother lives: yet whatsoe'er you do,
Fight and fight well; strike and strike home.   O dear
Brothers, the woman's Angel guards you, you
The sole men to be mingled with our cause,
The sole men we shall prize in the after-time,
Your very armour hallow'd, and your statues
Rear'd, sung to, when this gad-fly brush'd aside,
We plant a solid foot into the Time,
And mould a generation strong to move
With claim on claim from right to right, till she
Whose name is yoked with children's, know herself;
And Knowledge in our own land make her free,
And, ever following those two crowned twins,
Commerce and conquest, shower the fiery grain
Of freedom broadcast over all that orbs
Between the Northern and the Southern morn."

  Then came a postscript dash'd across the rest.
"See that there be no traitors in your camp:
We seem a nest of traitors — none to trust
Since our arms fail'd — this Egypt-plague of men!

Almost our maids were better at their homes,
Than thus man-girdled here: indeed I think
Our chiefest comfort is the little child
Of one unworthy mother; which she left:
She shall not have it back: the child shall grow
To prize the authentic mother of her mind.
I took it for an hour in mine own bed
This morning: there the tender orphan hands
Felt at my heart, and seem'd to charm from thence
The wrath I nursed against the world: farewell."

I ceased; he said: "Stubborn, but she may sit
Upon a king's right hand in thunder-storms,
And breed up warriors! See now, tho' yourself
Be dazzled by the wildfire Love to sloughs
That swallow common sense, the spindling king,
This Gama swamp'd in lazy tolerance.
When the man wants weight, the woman takes it up,
And topples down the scales; but this is fixt
As are the roots of earth and base of all;
Man for the field and woman for the hearth:
Man for the sword and for the needle she:
Man with the head and woman with the heart:
Man to command and woman to obey;
All else confusion. Look you! the gray mare
Is ill to live with, when her whinny shrills

From tile to scullery, and her small goodman
Shrinks in his arm-chair while the fires of Hell
Mix with his hearth: but you — she's yet a colt —
Take, break her: strongly groom'd and straitly curb'd
She might not rank with those detestable
That let the bantling scald at home, and brawl
Their rights or wrongs like potherbs in the street.
They say she's comely; there's the fairer chance:
I like her none the less for rating at her!
Besides, the woman wed is not as we,
But suffers change of frame.   A lusty brace
Of twins may weed her of her folly.   Boy,
The bearing and the training of a child
Is woman's wisdom."
                         Thus the hard old king:
I took my leave, for it was nearly noon:
I pored upon her letter which I held,
And on the little clause "take not his life:"
I mused on that wild morning in the woods,
And on the "Follow, follow, thou shalt win:"
I thought on all the wrathful king had said,
And how the strange betrothment was to end:
Then I remember'd that burnt sorcerer's curse
That one should fight with shadows and should fall;
And like a flash the weird affection came:
King, camp and college turn'd to hollow shows;
I seem'd to move in old memorial tilts,

And doing battle with forgotten ghosts,
To dream myself the shadow of a dream:
And ere I woke it was the point of noon,
The lists were ready. Empanoplied and plumed
We enter'd in, and waited, fifty there
Opposed to fifty, till the trumpet blared
At the barrier like a wild horn in a land
Of echoes, and a moment, and once more
The trumpet, and again; at which the storm
Of galloping hoofs bare on the ridge of spears
And riders front to front, until they closed
In conflict with the crash of shivering points,
And thunder. Yet it seem'd a dream, I dream'd
Of fighting. On his haunches rose the steed,
And into fiery splinters leapt the lance,
And out of stricken helmets sprang the fire.
Part sat like rocks: part reel'd but kept their seats:
Part roll'd on the earth and rose again and drew:
Part stumbled mixt with floundering horses. Down
From those two bulks at Arac's side, and down
From Arac's arm, as from a giant's flail,
The large blows rain'd, as here and everywhere
He rode the mellay, lord of the ringing lists,
And all the plain, — brand, mace, and shaft, and shield —
Shock'd, like an iron-clanging anvil bang'd
With hammers; till I thought, can this be he
From Gama's dwarfish loins? if this be so,

The mother makes us most — and in my dream
I glanced aside, and saw the palace-front
Alive with fluttering scarfs and ladies' eyes,
And highest, among the statues, statuelike,
Between a cymbal'd Miriam and a Jael,
With Psyche's babe, was Ida watching us,
A single band of gold about her hair,
Like a Saint's glory up in heaven: but she
No saint — inexorable — no tenderness —
Too hard, too cruel: yet she sees me fight,
Yea, let her see me fall! with that I drave
Among the thickest and bore down a Prince,
And Cyril, one.　Yea, let me make my dream
All that I would.　But that large-moulded man,
His visage all agrin as at a wake,
Made at me thro' the press, and, staggering back
With stroke on stroke the horse and horseman, came
As comes a pillar of electric cloud,
Flaying the roofs and sucking up the drains,
And shadowing down the champain till it strikes
On a wood, and takes, and breaks, and cracks, and splits,
And twists the grain with such a roar that Earth
Reels, and the herdsmen cry; for everything
Gave way before him: only Florian, he
That loved me closer than his own right eye,
Thrust in between; but Arac rode him down:
And Cyril seeing it, push'd against the Prince,

With Psyche's colour round his helmet, tough,
Strong, supple, sinew-corded, apt at arms;
But tougher, heavier, stronger, he that smote
And threw him: last I spurr'd; I felt my veins
Stretch with fierce heat; a moment hand to hand,
And sword to sword, and horse to horse we hung,
Till I struck out and shouted; the blade glanced;
I did but shear a feather, and dream and truth
Flow'd from me; darkness closed me; and I fell.

Home they brought her warrior dead:
  She nor swoon'd, nor utter'd cry:
All her maidens, watching, said,
  "She must weep or she will die."

Then they praised him, soft and low,
  Call'd him worthy to be loved,
Truest friend and noblest foe;
  Yet she neither spoke nor moved.

Stole a maiden from her place,
  Lightly to the warrior stept,
Took the face-cloth from the face;
  Yet she neither moved nor wept.

Rose a nurse of ninety years,
  Set his child upon her knee —
Like summer tempest came her tears —
  "Sweet my child, I live for thee."

VI

My dream had never died or lived again.
As in some mystic middle state I lay;
Seeing I saw not, hearing not I heard:
Tho', if I saw not, yet they told me all
So often that I speak as having seen.

For so it seem'd, or so they said to me,
That all things grew more tragic and more strange;
'That when our side was vanquish'd and my cause
For ever lost, there went up a great cry,
The Prince is slain. My father heard and ran
In on the lists, and there unlaced my casque
And grovell'd on my body, and after him
Came Psyche, sorrowing for Aglaïa.
But high upon the palace Ida stood
With Psyche's babe in arm: there on the roofs
Like that great dame of Lapidoth she sang.

"Our enemies have fall'n, have fall'n: the seed
The little seed they laugh'd at in the dark,
Has risen and cleft the soil, and grown a bulk
Of spanless girth, that lays on every side
A thousand arms and rushes to the Sun.

"Our enemies have fall'n, have fall'n: they came;
The leaves were wet with women's tears: they heard

A noise of songs they would not understand:
They mark'd it with the red cross to the fall,
And would have strown it, and are fall'n themselves.

    "Our enemies have fall'n, have fall'n: they came,
The woodmen with their axes: lo the tree!
But we will make it faggots for the hearth,
And shape it plank and beam for roof and floor,
And boats and bridges for the use of men.

    "Our enemies have fall'n, have fall'n: they struck;
With their own blows they hurt themselves, nor knew
There dwelt an iron nature in the grain:
The glittering axe was broken in their arms,
Their arms were shatter'd to the shoulder blade.

    "Our enemies have fall'n, but this shall grow
A night of Summer from the heat, a breadth
Of Autumn, dropping fruits of power; and roll'd
With music in the growing breeze of Time,
The tops shall strike from star to star, the fangs
Shall move the stony bases of the world.

    "And now, O maids, behold our sanctuary
Is violate, our laws broken: fear we not
To break them more in their behoof, whose arms
Champion'd our cause and won it with a day
Blanch'd in our annals, and perpetual feast,

When dames and heroines of the golden year
Shall strip a hundred hollows bare of Spring,
To rain an April of ovation round
Their statues, borne aloft, the three: but come,
We will be liberal, since our rights are won.
Let them not lie in the tents with coarse mankind,
Ill nurses; but descend, and proffer these
The brethren of our blood and cause, that there
Lie bruised and maim'd, the tender ministries
Of female hands and hospitality."

She spoke, and with the babe yet in her arms,
Descending, burst the great bronze valves, and led
A hundred maids in train across the Park.
Some cowl'd, and some bare-headed, on they came,
Their feet in flowers, her loveliest: by them went
The enamour'd air sighing, and on their curls
From the high tree the blossom wavering fell,
And over them the tremulous isles of light
Slided, they moving under shade: but Blanche
At distance follow'd: so they came: anon
Thro' open field into the lists they wound
Timorously; and as the leader of the herd
That holds a stately fretwork to the Sun,
And follow'd up by a hundred airy does,
Steps with a tender foot, light as on air,
The lovely, lordly creature floated on
To where her wounded brethren lay; there stay'd;

Knelt on one knee, — the child on one, — and prest
Their hands, and call'd them dear deliverers,
And happy warriors, and immortal names,
And said "You shall not lie in the tents but here,
And nursed by those for whom you fought, and served
With female hands and hospitality."

Then, whether moved by this, or was it chance,
She past my way. Up started from my side
The old lion, glaring with his whelpless eye,
Silent; but when she saw me lying stark,
Dishelm'd and mute, and motionlessly pale,
Cold ev'n to her, she sigh'd; and when she saw
The haggard father's face and reverend beard
Of grisly twine, all, dabbled with the blood
Of his own son, shudder'd, a twitch of pain
Tortured her mouth, and o'er her forehead past
A shadow, and her hue changed, and she said:
"He saved my life: my brother slew him for it"
No more: at which the king in bitter scorn
Drew from my neck the painting and the tress,
And held them up: she saw them, and a day
Rose from the distance on her memory,
When the good Queen, her mother, shore the tress
With kisses, ere the days of Lady Blanche:
And then once more she look'd at my pale face:
Till understanding all the foolish work
Of Fancy, and the bitter close of all,

Her iron will was broken in her mind;
Her noble heart was molten in her breast;
She bow'd, she set the child on the earth; she laid
A feeling finger on my brows, and presently
"O Sire," she said, "he lives: he is not dead:
O let me have him with my brethren here
In our own palace: we will tend on him
Like one of these; if so, by any means,
To lighten this great clog of thanks, that make
Our progress falter to the woman's goal."

    She said: but at the happy word "he lives"
My father stoop'd, re-father'd o'er my wounds.
So those two foes above my fallen life,
With brow to brow like night and evening mixt
Their dark and gray, while Psyche ever stole
A little nearer, till the babe that by us,
Half-lapt in glowing gauze and golden brede,
Lay like a new-fall'n meteor on the grass,
Uncared for, spied its mother and began
A blind and babbling laughter, and to dance
Its body, and reach its fatling innocent arms
And lazy lingering fingers. She the appeal
Brook'd not, but clamouring out "Mine — mine — not
            yours,
It is not yours, but mine: give me the child"
Ceased all on tremble: piteous was the cry:
So stood the unhappy mother open-mouth'd,
                                    18*

And turn'd each face her way: wan was her cheek
With hollow watch, her blooming mantle torn,
Red grief and mother's hunger in her eye,
And down dead-heavy sank her curls, and half
The sacred mother's bosom, panting, burst
The laces toward her babe; but she nor cared
Nor knew it, clamouring on, till Ida heard,
Look'd up, and rising slowly from me, stood
Erect and silent, striking with her glance
The mother, me, the child; but he that lay
Beside us, Cyril, batter'd as he was,
Trail'd himself up on one knee: then he drew
Her robe to meet his lips, and down she look'd
At the arm'd man sideways, pitying, as it seem'd,
Or self-involved; but when she learnt his face,
Remembering his ill-omen'd song, arose
Once more thro' all her height, and o'er him grew
Tall as a figure lengthen'd on the sand
When the tide ebbs in sunshine, and he said:

"O fair and strong and terrible! Lioness
That with your long locks play the Lion's mane!
But Love and Nature, these are two more terrible
And stronger. See, your foot is on our necks,
We vanquish'd, you the Victor of your will.
What would you more? give her the child! remain
Orb'd in your isolation: he is dead,
Or all as dead: henceforth we let you be:

Win you the hearts of women; and beware
Lest, where you seek the common love of these,
The common hate with the revolving wheel
Should drag you down, and some great Nemesis
Break from a darken'd future, crown'd with fire,
And tread you out for ever: but howsoe'er
Fix'd in yourself, never in your own arms
To hold your own, deny not her's to her,
Give her the child! O if, I say, you keep
One pulse that beats true woman, if you loved
The breast that fed or arm that dandled you,
Or own one part of sense not flint to prayer,
Give her the child! or if you scorn to lay it,
Yourself, in hands so lately claspt with yours,
Or speak to her, your dearest, her one fault
The tenderness, not yours, that could not kill,
Give *me* it; *I* will give it her."

                       He said:
At first her eye with slow dilation roll'd
Dry flame, she listening; after sank and sank
And, into mournful twilight mellowing, dwelt
Full on the child; she took it: "Pretty bud!
Lily of the vale! half open'd bell of the woods!
Sole comfort of my dark hour, when a world
Of traitorous friend and broken system made
No purple in the distance, mystery,
Pledge of a love not to be mine, farewell;
These men are hard upon us as of old,

We two must part: and yet how fain was I
To dream thy cause embraced in mine, to think
I might be something to thee, when I felt
Thy helpless warmth about my barren breast
In the dead prime: but may thy mother prove
As true to thee as false, false, false to me!
And, if thou needs must bear the yoke, I wish it
Gentle as freedom" — here she kiss'd it: then —
"All good go with thee! take it Sir" and so
Laid the soft babe in his hard-mailed hands,
Who turn'd half-round to Psyche as she sprang
To meet it, with an eye that swum in thanks;
Then felt it sound' and whole from head to foot,
And hugg'd and never hugg'd it close enough,
And in her hunger mouth'd and mumbled it,
And hid her bosom with it; after that
Put on more calm and added suppliantly;

"We two were friends: I go to mine own land
For ever: find some other: as for me
I scarce am fit for your great plans: yet speak to me,
Say one soft word and let me part forgiven."

But Ida spoke not, rapt upon the child.
Then Arac. "Ida — 'sdeath! you blame the man;
You wrong yourselves — the woman is so hard
Upon the woman. Come, a grace to me!
I am your warrior: I and mine have fought

Your battle: kiss her; take her hand, she weeps:
'Sdeath! I would sooner fight thrice o'er than see it."

But Ida spoke not, gazing on the ground,
And reddening in the furrows of his chin,
And moved beyond his custom, Gama said:

"I've heard that there is iron in the blood,
And I believe it. Not one word? not one?
Whence drew you this steel temper? not from me,
Not from your mother now a saint with saints.
She said you had a heart — I heard her say it —
'Our Ida has a heart' — just ere she died —
'But see that some one with authority
Be near her still' and I — I sought for one —
All people said she had authority —
The Lady Blanche: much profit! Not one word;
No! tho' your father sues: see how you stand
Stiff as Lot's wife, and all the good knights maim'd,
I trust that there is no one hurt to death,
For your wild whim: and was it then for this,
Was it for this we gave our palace up,
Where we withdrew from summer heats and state,
And had our wine and chess beneath the planes,
And many a pleasant hour with her that's gone,
Ere you were born to vex us? Is it kind?
Speak to her I say: is this not she of whom,
When first she came, all flush'd you said to me

Now had you got a friend of your own age,
Now could you share your thought; now should men see
Two women faster welded in one love
Than pairs of wedlock; she you walk'd with, she
You talk'd with, whole nights long, up in the tower,
Of sine and arc, spheroïd and azimuth,
And right ascension, Heaven knows what; and now
A word, but one, one little kindly word,
Not one to spare her: out upon you, flint!
You love nor her, nor me, nor any; nay,
You shame your mother's judgement too.   Not one?
You will not? well — no heart have you, or such
As fancies like the vermin in a nut
Have fretted all to dust and bitterness."
So said the small king moved beyond his wont.

     But Ida stood nor spoke, drain'd of her force
By many a varying influence and so long.
Down thro' her limbs a drooping languor wept:
Her head a little bent; and on her mouth
A doubtful smile dwelt like a clouded moon
In a still water: then brake out my sire
Lifting his grim head from my wounds.   "O you,
Woman, whom we thought woman even now,
And were half fool'd to let you tend our son,
Because he might have wish'd it — but we see
The accomplice of your madness unforgiven,
And think that you might mix his draught with death,

When your skies change again: the rougher hand
Is safer: on to the tents: take up the Prince."

He rose, and while each ear was prick'd to attend
A tempest, thro' the cloud that dimm'd her broke
A genial warmth and light once more, and shone
Thro' glittering drops on her sad friend.

                                "Come hither,
O Psyche," she cried out, "embrace me, come,
Quick while I melt; make reconcilement sure
With one that cannot keep her mind an hour:
Come to the hollow heart they slander so!
Kiss and be friends, like children being chid!
I seem no more: *I* want forgiveness too:
I should have had to do with none but maids,
That have no links with men.   Ah false but dear,
Dear traitor, too much loved, why? — why? — Yet see,
Before these kings we embrace you yet once more
With all forgiveness, all oblivion,
And trust, not love, you less.

                            And now, O Sire,
Grant me your son, to nurse, to wait upon him,
Like mine own brother.   For my debt to him,
This nightmare weight of gratitude, I know it;
Taunt me no more: yourself and yours shall have
Free adit; we will scatter all our maids
'Till happier times each to her proper hearth:
What use to keep them here now? grant my prayer.

Help, father, brother, help; speak to the king:
Thaw this male nature to some touch of that
Which kills me with myself, and drags me down
From my fixt height to mob me up with all
The soft and milky rabble of womankind,
Poor weakling ev'n as they are."

                                        Passionate tears
Follow'd: the king replied not: Cyril said:
"Your brother, Lady, — Florian, — ask for him
Of your great head — for he is wounded too —
That you may tend upon him with the prince."
"Ay so," said Ida with a bitter smile,
"Our laws are broken: let him enter too."
Then Violet, she that sang the mournful song,
And had a cousin tumbled on the plain,
Petition'd too for him. "Ay so," she said,
"I stagger in the stream: I cannot keep
My heart an eddy from the brawling hour:
We break our laws with ease, but let it be."
"Ay so?" said Blanche: "Amazed am I to hear
Your Highness: but your Highness breaks with ease
The law your Highness did not make: 'twas I.
I had been wedded wife, I knew mankind,
And block'd them out; but these men came to woo
Your Highness — verily I think to win."

    So she: and turn'd askance a wintry eye,
But Ida with a voice, that like a bell

Toll'd by an earthquake in a trembling tower,
Rang ruin, answer'd full of grief and scorn.

   "Fling our doors wide! all, all, not one, but all,
Not only he, but by my mother's soul,
Whatever man lies wounded, friend or foe,
Shall enter, if he will. Let our girls flit,
Till the storm die! but had you stood by us,
The roar that breaks the Pharos from his base
Had left us rock. She fain would sting us too,
But shall not. Pass, and mingle with your likes.
We brook no further insult but are gone."

   She turn'd; the very nape of her white neck
Was rosed with indignation: but the Prince
Her brother came; the king her father charm'd
Her wounded soul with words: nor did mine own
Refuse her proffer, lastly gave his hand.

   Then us they lifted up, dead weights, and bare
Straight to the doors: to them the doors gave way
Groaning, and in the Vestal entry shriek'd
The virgin marble under iron heels:
And on they moved and gain'd the hall, and there
Rested: but great the crush was, and each base,
To left and right, of those tall columns drown'd
In silken fluctuation and the swarm
Of female whisperers: at the further end

Was Ida by the throne, the two great cats
Close by her, like supporters on a shield,
Bow-back'd with fear: but in the centre stood
The common men with rolling eyes; amazed
They glared upon the women, and aghast
The women stared at these, all silent, save
When armour clash'd or jingled, while the day,
Descending, struck athwart the hall, and shot
A flying splendour out of brass and steel,
That o'er the statues leapt from head to head,
Now fired an angry Pallas on the helm,
Now set a wrathful Dian's moon on flame,
And now and then an echo started up,
And shuddering fled from room to room, and died
Of fright in far apartments.
                              Then the voice
Of Ida sounded, issuing ordinance:
And me they bore up the broad stairs, and thro'
The long-laid galleries past a hundred doors
To one deep chamber shut from sound, and due
To languid limbs and sickness; left me in it;
And others otherwhere they laid; and all
That afternoon a sound arose of hoof
And chariot, many a maiden passing home
Till happier times; but some were left of those
Held sagest, and the great lords out and in,
From those two hosts that lay beside the walls,
Walk'd at their will, and everything was changed.

Ask me no more: the moon may draw the sea;
  The cloud may stoop from heaven and take the shape,
  With fold to fold, of mountain or of cape;
But O too fond, when have I answer'd thee?
       Ask me no more.

Ask me no more: what answer should I give?
  I love not hollow cheek or faded eye:
  Yet, O my friend, I will not have thee die!
Ask me no more, lest I should bid thee live;
       Ask me no more.

Ask me no more: thy fate and mine are seal'd:
  I strove against the stream and all in vain:
  Let the great river take me to the main:
No more, dear love, for at a touch I yield;
       Ask me no more.

So was their sanctuary violated,
So their fair college turn'd to hospital;
At first with all confusion: by and bye
Sweet order lived again with other laws:
A kindlier influence reign'd; and everywhere
Low voices with the ministering hand
Hung round the sick: the maidens came, they talk'd,
They sang, they read: till she not fair, began
To gather light, and she that was, became
Her former beauty treble; and to and fro
With books, with flowers, with Angel offices,
Like creatures native unto gracious act,
And in their own clear element, they moved.

But sadness on the soul of Ida fell,
And hatred of her weakness, blent with shame.
Old studies fail'd; seldom she spoke; but oft
Clomb to the roofs, and gazed alone for hours
On that disastrous leaguer, swarms of men
Darkening her female field: void was her use;
And she as one that climbs a peak to gaze
O'er land and main, and sees a great black cloud
Drag inward from the deeps, a wall of night,
Blot out the slope of sea from verge to shore,

And suck the blinding splendour from the sand,
And quenching lake by lake and tarn by tarn
Expunge the world: so fared she gazing there;
So blacken'd all her world in secret, blank
And waste it seem'd and vain; till down she came,
And found fair peace once more among the sick.

And twilight dawn'd; and morn by morn the lark
Shot up and shrill'd in flickering gyres, but I
Lay silent in the muffled cage of life:
And twilight gloom'd; and broader-grown the bowers
Drew the great night into themselves, and Heaven,
Star after star, arose and fell; but I,
Deeper than those weird doubts could reach me, lay
Quite sunder'd from the moving Universe,
Nor knew what eye was on me, nor the hand
That nursed me, more than infants in their sleep.

But Psyche tended Florian: with her oft
Melissa came; for Blanche had gone, but left
Her child among us, willing she should keep
Court-favour: here and there the small bright head,
A light of healing, glanced about the couch,
Or thro' the parted silks the tender face
Peep'd, shining in upon the wounded man
With blush and smile, a medicine in themselves
To wile the length from languorous hours, and draw
The sting from pain; nor seem'd it strange that soon

He rose up whole, and those fair charities
Join'd at her side; nor stranger seem'd that hearts
So gentle, so employ'd, should close in love,
Than when two dewdrops on the petal shake
To the same sweet air, and tremble deeper down,
And slip at once all-fragrant into one.

Less prosperously the second suit obtain'd
At first with Psyche. Not tho' Blanche had sworn
That after that dark night among the fields,
She needs must wed him for her own good name;
Not tho' he built upon the babe restored;
Nor tho' she liked him, yielded she, but fear'd
To incense the Head once more; till on a day
When Cyril pleaded, Ida came behind
Seen but of Psyche: on her foot she hung
A moment, and she heard, at which her face
A little flush'd, and she past on; but each
Assumed from thence a half-consent involved
In stillness, plighted troth, and were at peace.

Nor only these: Love in the sacred halls
Held carnival at will, and flying struck
With showers of random sweet on maid and man.
Nor did her father cease to press my claim,
Nor did mine own now reconciled; nor yet
Did those twin brothers, risen again and whole;
Nor Arac, satiate with his victory.

But I lay still, and with me oft she sat:
Then came a change; for sometimes I would catch
Her hand in wild delirium, gripe it hard,
And fling it like a viper off, and shriek
"You are not Ida;" clasp it once again,
And call her Ida, tho' I knew her not,
And call her sweet, as if in irony,
And call her hard and cold which seem'd a truth:
And still she fear'd that I should lose my mind,
And often she believed that I should die:
Till out of long frustration of her care,
And pensive tendance in the all-weary noons,
And watches in the dead, the dark, when clocks
Throbb'd thunder thro' the palace floors, or call'd
On flying Time from all their silver tongues —
And out of memories of her kindlier days,
And sidelong glances at my father's grief,
And at the happy lovers heart in heart —
And out of hauntings of my spoken love,
And lonely listenings to my mutter'd dream,
And often feeling of the helpless hands,
And wordless broodings on the wasted cheek —
From all a closer interest flourish'd up,
Tenderness touch by touch, and last, to these,
Love, like an Alpine harebell hung with tears
By some cold morning glacier; frail at first
And feeble, all unconscious of itself,
But such as gather'd colour day by day.

Last I woke sane, but well-nigh close to death
For weakness: it was evening: silent light
Slept on the painted walls, wherein were wrought
Two grand designs; for on one side arose
The women up in wild revolt, and storm'd
At the Oppian law. Titanic shapes, they cramm'd
The forum, and half-crush'd among the rest
A dwarflike Cato cower'd. On the other side
Hortensia spoke against the tax; behind,
A train of dames: by axe and eagle sat,
With all their foreheads drawn in Roman scowls,
And half the wolf's-milk curdled in their veins,
The fierce triumvirs; and before them paused
Hortensia, pleading: angry was her face.

I saw the forms: I knew not where I was:
They did but look like hollow shows; nor more
Sweet Ida: palm to palm she sat: the dew
Dwelt in her eyes, and softer all her shape
And rounder seem'd: I moved: I sigh'd: a touch
Came round my wrist, and tears upon my hand:
Then all for languor and self-pity ran
Mine down my face, and with what life I had,
And like a flower that cannot all unfold,
So drench'd it is with tempest, to the sun,
Yet, as it may, turns toward him, I on her
Fixt my faint eyes, and utter'd whisperingly:

"If you be, what I think you, some sweet dream,
I would but ask you to fulfil yourself:
But if you be that Ida whom I knew,
I ask you nothing: only, if a dream,
Sweet dream,' be perfect. I shall die to-night.
Stoop down and seem to kiss me ere I die."

I could no more, but lay like one in trance,
That hears his burial talk'd of by his friends,
And cannot speak, nor move, nor make one sign,
But lies and dreads his doom. She turn'd; she paused;
She stoop'd; and out of languor leapt a cry;
Leapt fiery Passion from the brinks of death;
And I believed that in the living world
My spirit closed with Ida's at the lips;
Till back I fell, and from mine arms she rose
Glowing all over noble shame; and all
Her falser self slipt from her like a robe,
And left her woman, lovelier in her mood
Than in her mould that other, when she came
From barren deeps to conquer all with love;
And down the streaming crystal dropt; and she
Far-fleeted by the purple island-sides,
Naked, a double light in air and wave,
To meet her Graces, where they deck'd her out
For worship without end; nor end of mine,
Stateliest, for thee! but mute she glided forth,

Nor glanced behind her, and I sank and slept,
Fill'd thro' and thro' with Love, a happy sleep.

Deep in the night I woke: she, near me, held
A volume of the Poets of her land:
There to herself, all in low tones, she read.

"Now sleeps the crimson petal, now the white;
Nor waves the cypress in the palace walk;
Nor winks the gold fin in the porphyry font:
The fire-fly wakens: waken thou with me.

Now droops the milkwhite peacock like a ghost,
And like a ghost she glimmers on to me.

Now lies the Earth all Danaë to the stars,
And all thy heart lies open unto me.

Now slides the silent meteor on, and leaves
A shining furrow, as thy thoughts in me.

Now folds the lily all her sweetness up,
And slips into the bosom of the lake:
So fold thyself, my dearest, thou, and slip
Into my bosom and be lost in me."

I heard her turn the page; she found a small
Sweet Idyl, and once more, as low, she read:

"Come down, O maid, from yonder mountain height:
What pleasure lives in height (the shepherd sang)
In height and cold, the splendour of the hills?
But cease to move so near the Heavens, and cease
To glide a sunbeam by the blasted Pine,
To sit a star upon the sparkling spire;
And come, for Love is of the valley, come
For Love is of the valley, come thou down
And find him; by the happy threshold, he,
Or hand in hand with Plenty in the maize,
Or red with spirted purple of the vats,
Or foxlike in the vine; nor cares to walk
With Death and Morning on the silver horns,
Nor wilt thou snare him in the white ravine,
Nor find him dropt upon the firths of ice,
That huddling slant in furrow-cloven falls
To roll the torrent out of dusky doors:
But follow; let the torrent dance thee down
To find him in the valley; let the wild
Lean-headed Eagles yelp alone, and leave
The monstrous ledges there to slope, and spill
Their thousand wreaths of dangling water-smoke,
That like a broken purpose waste in air:
So waste not thou; but come; for all the vales
Await thee; azure pillars of the hearth
Arise to thee; the children call, and I
Thy shepherd pipe, and sweet is every sound,
Sweeter thy voice, but every sound is sweet;

Myriads of rivulets hurryiug thro' the lawn,
The moan of doves in immemorial elms,
And murmuring of innumerable bees."

So she low-toned; while with shut eyes I lay
Listening; then look'd.   Pale was the perfect face;
The bosom with long sighs labour'd; and meek
Seem'd the full lips, and mild the luminous eyes,
And the voice trembled and the hand.   She said
Brokenly, that she knew it, she had fail'd
In sweet humility; had fail'd in all;
That all her labour was but as a block
Left in the quarry; but she still were loth,
She still were loth to yield herself to one,
That wholly scorn'd to help their equal rights
Against the sons of men, and barbarous laws.
She pray'd me not to judge their cause from her
That wrong'd it, sought far less for truth than power
In knowledge: something wild within her breast,
A greater than all knowledge, beat her down.
And she had nursed me there from week to week:
Much had she learnt in little time.   In part
It was ill counsel had misled the girl
To vex true hearts: yet was she but a girl —
"Ah fool, and made myself a Queen of farce!
When comes another such? never, I think,
Till the Sun drop dead from the signs."

                              Her voice

Choked, and her forehead sank upon her hands,
And her great heart thro' all the faultful Past
Went sorrowing in a pause I dared not break;
Till notice of a change in the dark world
Was lispt about the acacias, and a bird,
That early woke to feed her little ones,
Sent from a dewy breast a cry for light:
She moved, and at her feet the volume fell.

"Blame not thyself too much," I said, "nor blame
Too much the sons of men and barbarous laws;
These were the rough ways of the world till now.
Henceforth thou hast a helper, me, that know
The woman's cause is man's: they rise or sink
Together, dwarf'd or godlike, bond or free:
For she that out of Lethe scales with man
The shining steps of Nature, shares with man
His nights, his days, moves with him to one goal,
Stays all the fair young planet in her hands —
If she be small, slight-natured, miserable,
How shall men grow? but work no more alone!
Our place is much: as far as in us lies
We two will serve them both in aiding her —
Will clear away the parasitic forms
That seem to keep her up but drag her down —
Will leave her space to burgeon out of all
Within her — let her make herself her own
To give or keep, to live and learn and be

All that not harms distinctive womanhood.
For woman is not undevelopt man,
But diverse: could we make her as the man,
Sweet Love were slain: his dearest bond is this,
Not like to like, but like in difference.
Yet in the long years liker must they grow;
The man be more of woman, she of man;
He gain in sweetness and in moral height,
Nor lose the wrestling thews that throw the world;
She mental breadth, nor fail in childward care,
Nor lose the childlike in the larger mind;
Till at the last she set herself to man,
Like perfect music unto noble words;
And so these twain, upon the skirts of Time,
Sit side by side, full-summ'd in all their powers,
Dispensing harvest, sowing the To-be,
Self-reverent each and reverencing each,
Distinct in individualities,
But like each other ev'n as those who love.
Then comes the statelier Eden back to men:
Then reign the world's great bridals, chaste and calm:
Then springs the crowning race of humankind.
May these things be!"

       Sighing she spoke "I fear
They will not."

       "Dear, but let us type them now
In our own lives, and this proud watchword rest
Of equal; seeing either sex alone

Is half itself, and in true marriage lies
Nor equal, nor unequal: each fulfils
Defect in each, and always thought in thought,
Purpose in purpose, will in will, they grow,
The single pure and perfect animal,
The two-cell'd heart beating, with one full stroke,
Life."
   And again sighing she spoke: "A dream
That once was mine! what woman taught you this?"

"Alone" I said "from earlier than I know,
Immersed in rich foreshadowings of the world,
I loved the woman: he, that doth not, lives
A drowning life, besotted in sweet self,
Or pines in sad experience worse than death,
Or keeps his wing'd affections clipt with crime:
Yet was there one thro' whom I loved her, one
Not learned, save in gracious household ways,
Not perfect, nay, but full of tender wants,
No Angel, but a dearer being, all dipt
In Angel instincts, breathing Paradise,
Interpreter between the Gods and men,
Who look'd all native to her place, and yet
On tiptoe seem'd to touch upon a sphere
Too gross to tread, and all male minds perforce
Sway'd to her from their orbits as they moved,
And girdled her with music.   Happy he
With such a mother! faith in womankind

Beats with his blood, and trust in all things high
Comes easy to him, and tho' he trip and fall
He shall not blind his soul with clay."
                                    "But I,"
Said Ida, tremulously, "so all unlike —
It seems you love to cheat yourself with words:
This mother is your model. I have heard
Of your strange doubts: they well might be: I seem
A mockery to my own self. Never, Prince;
You cannot love me."
                        "Nay but thee" I said
"From yearlong poring on thy pictured eyes,
Ere seen I loved, and loved thee seen, and saw
Thee woman thro' the crust of iron moods
That mask'd thee from men's reverence up, and forced
Sweet love on pranks of saucy boyhood: now,
Giv'n back to life, to life indeed, thro' thee,
Indeed I love: the new day comes, the light
Dearer for night, as dearer thou for faults
Lived over: lift thine eyes; my doubts are dead,
My haunting sense of hollow shows: the change,
This truthful change in thee has kill'd it. Dear,
Look up, and let thy nature strike on mine,
Like yonder morning on the blind half-world;
Approach and fear not; breathe upon my brows;
In that fine air I tremble, all the past
Melts mist-like into this bright hour, and this
Is morn to more, and all the rich to-come

Reels, as the golden Autumn woodland reels
Athwart the smoke of burning weeds.   Forgive me,
I waste my heart in signs: let be.   My bride,
My wife, my life.   O we will walk this world,
Yoked in all exercise of noble end,
And so thro' those dark gates across the wild
That no man knows.   Indeed I love thee: come,
Yield thyself up: my hopes and thine are one:
Accomplish thou my manhood and thyself;
Lay thy sweet hands in mine and trust to me."

CONCLUSION.

So closed our tale, of which I give you all
The random scheme as wildly as it rose:
The words are mostly mine; for when we ceased
There came a minute's pause, and Walter said,
"I wish she had not yielded!" then to me,
"What, if you drest it up poetically!"
So pray'd the men, the women: I gave assent:
Yet how to bind the scatter'd scheme of seven
Together in one sheaf? What style could suit?
The men required that I should give throughout
The sort of mock-heroic gigantesque,
With which we banter'd little Lilia first:
The women — and perhaps they felt their power,
For something in the ballads which they sang,
Or in their silent influence as they sat,
Had ever seem'd to wrestle with burlesque,
And drove us, last, to quite a solemn close —
They hated banter, wish'd for something real,
A gallant fight, a noble princess — why
Not make her true-heroic — true sublime?
Or all, they said, as earnest as the close?

Which yet with such a framework scarce could be.
Then rose a little feud betwixt the two,
Betwixt the mockers and the realists:
And I, betwixt them both to please them both,
And yet to give the story as it rose,
I moved as in a strange diagonal,
And maybe neither pleased myself nor them.

But Lilia pleased me, for she took no part
In our dispute: the sequel of the tale
Had touch'd her; and she sat, she pluck'd the grass,
She flung it from her, thinking: last, she fixt
A showery glance upon her aunt, and said,
"You — tell us what we are" who might have told,
For she was cramm'd with theories out of books,
But that there rose a shout: the gates were closed
At sunset, and the crowd were swarming now,
To take their leave, about the garden rails.

So I and some went out to these: we climb'd
The slope to Vivian-place, and turning saw
The happy valleys, half in light, and half
Far-shadowing from the west, a land of peace;
Gray halls alone among their massive groves;
Trim hamlets; here and there a rustic tower
Half-lost in belts of hop and breadths of wheat;

The shimmering glimpses of a stream; the seas;
A red sail, or a white; and far beyond,
Imagined more than seen, the skirts of France.

    "Look there, a garden!" said my college friend,
The Tory member's elder son "and there!
God bless the narrow sea which keeps her off,
And keeps our Britain, whole within herself,
A nation yet, the rulers and the ruled —
Some sense of duty, something of a faith,
Some reverence for the laws ourselves have made,
Some patient force to change them when we will,
Some civic manhood firm against the crowd —
But yonder, whiff! there comes a sudden heat,
The gravest citizen seems to lose his head,
The king is scared, the soldier will not fight,
The little boys begin to shoot and stab,
A kingdom topples over with a shriek
Like an old woman, and down rolls the world
In mock heroics stranger than our own;
Revolts, republics, revolutions, most
No graver than a schoolboys' barring out;
Too comic for the solemn things they are,
Too solemn for the comic touches in them,
Like our wild Princess with as wise a dream
As some of theirs — God bless the narrow seas!
I wish they were a whole Atlantic broad."
"Have patience," I replied, "ourselves are full

Of social wroug; and maybe wildest dreams
Are but the needful preludes of the truth:
For me, the genial day, the happy crowd,
The sport half-science, fill me with a faith.
This fine old world of ours is but a child
Yet in the go-cart. Patience! Give it time
To learn its limbs: there is a hand that guides."

In such discourse we gain'd the garden rails,
And there we saw Sir Walter where he stood,
Before a tower of crimson holly-oaks,
Among six boys, head under head, and look'd
No little lily-handed Baronet he,
A great broad-shoulder'd genial Englishman,
A lord of fat prize-oxen and of sheep,
A raiser of huge melons and of pine,
A patron of some thirty charities,
A pamphleteer on guano and on grain,
A quarter-sessions chairman, abler none;
Fair-hair'd and redder than a windy morn;
Now shaking hands with him, now him, of those
That stood the nearest — now address'd to speech —
Who spoke few words and pithy, such as closed
Welcome, farewell, and welcome for the year
To follow: a shout rose again, and made
The long line of the approaching rookery swerve
From the elms, and shook the branches of the deer
From slope to slope thro' distant ferns, and rang

Beyond the bourn of sunset; O, a shout
More joyful than the city-roar that hails
Premier or king! Why should not these great Sirs
Give up their parks some dozen times a year
To let the people breathe? So thrice they cried,
I likewise, and in groups they stream'd away.

But we went back to the Abbey, and sat on,
So much the gathering darkness charm'd: we sat
But spoke not, rapt in nameless reverie,
Perchance upon the future man: the walls
Blacken'd about us, bats wheel'd and owls whoop'd,
And gradually the powers of the night,
That range above the region of the wind,
Deepening the courts of twilight broke them up
Thro' all the silent spaces of the worlds,
Beyond all thought into the Heaven of Heavens.

Last little Lilia, rising quietly,
Disrobed the glimmering statue of Sir Ralph
From those rich silks, and home well-pleased we went.

END OF VOL. II.

PRINTING OFFICE OF THE PUBLISHER.